JESSICA WATKINS PRESENTS

BAD, BUT
Perfectly
GOOD
At It 2

JASMINE WILLIAMS

Dedication:

This book is dedicated to each and everyone that has supported my vision and made it come to life. I love you all and I can't thank you enough for the amazing support I have received.

CHAPTER ONE
London

"Are you sure that you didn't shoot your father with another gun and get rid of it before we got to the scene?"

"If I got rid of one gun, then why wouldn't I have gotten rid of the other? When did I even have time to get rid of a gun when my mother was tied up and my sister was shot? Why would I leave them? Furthermore, why the hell are you trying so hard to make me the killer? Trying to make your job a little easier, huh? Well, you're going to have to work a little bit harder, Detective, because you got the wrong one." I sat back and folded my arms across my chest.

The blonde hair blue-eyed detective leaned over the table in the interrogation room and stared me down. He wore an irritated look on his face, but I didn't care. I was sick of being there because I knew that I hadn't killed anyone.

He stood up and started pacing back and forth in front of me. "I don't know, London, you tell me. I'm the one asking the questions here. From what I'm hearing, you had a motive to kill your father. He had your pregnant mother tied up didn't he? He had shot your sister. Maybe you feared for your own life and wanted to try and protect your family."

I shifted my hips in my seat because that hard chair had my ass hurting. "I said I didn't do anything! Look, am I under arrest? Because if not, then I'm out of here. You don't have a damn thing to hold me for. Y'all dragged me down here and put me in the system just to find out that the gun you found is legally registered to me. Not only that, but it wasn't even the same weapon used to shoot that piece of shit."

"Her story checks out. Looks like you're free to go, London," the female detective walked in and eyed her partner with evil eyes. "If you find out anything else, give us a call."

I stood up and glared at the white man for a moment before I spun on my heels and walked out of the room without saying a word. I was pissed off for having to go through all that bullshit, and I didn't even pull a trigger. So what I had a gun and it was found at the scene. *I* didn't use that motherfucker. I probably should have just told them the truth in the first place, but I was too busy trying to get to my baby sis, Tiana.

When I walked out of the precinct, my friend, Ty, was waiting for me in her black Acura. I had called her and asked her to pick me up from the precinct since my car was still at the hospital. When I hopped in the car, she didn't even wait five seconds before she started questioning me.

"What the hell you doing down here at the jail, bitch? What type of trouble your goody two shoe ass done got yourself into?"

I looked over at her and tried not to laugh out loud as I thought about how much she reminded me of Craig's girlfriend from the movie "Friday." She had the long blonde Poetic Justice style braids, long fingernails with a different design on each finger, and she was smacking on a piece of gum like it was her last meal. She was a pretty light skin girl, but ghetto was her middle name. Ty was the definition of a hood chick, but I loved her crazy ass.

"London! I know you hear me!"

"Girl, it's a long story." I tried to avoid the conversation all together but Ty was not letting it go that easily.

"I got all day." She looked at her watch like she had all the time in the world.

"You remember I told you about all the threats my mama has been getting lately? Well, it turns out we were wrong about it being Chief. The whole time it was my bitch ass dad—"

"Wait a minute. Time out, bitch!" Ty cut me off. "Did you just say your *daddy?* What type of shit?"

"Let me finish, girl! So I woke up to a bunch of missed calls and text messages from Tiana, and I knew right then and there that something was wrong. When I got home I find my mama tied to a chair, and Tiana and my dad had each other at gunpoint."

"Oh hell nah! So what did you do?"

I rolled my eyes and sucked my teeth. "Do you wanna talk or let me tell the damn story?"

"Okay, okay, girl! Damn! You ain't gotta be so rude."

"Well, shut the hell up then! And why are we still sitting here? What? You can't drive and listen at the same time? Multitask, bitch!" We shared a laugh before she put the car in reverse and backed out of the space.

"Now let me get back to what I was saying. I pulled my gun out and got ready to bust at him." I looked over at Ty, and she looked like she was dying to say something. "The only thing that stopped me was the fact that he aimed his gun at my mom. I knew that if one of us shot him, my mom would have been taking a bullet to the head. So long story short: My dad shot Tiana, and as soon as he let off the shot, somebody came through and shot that bitch ass nigga in the dome and he died. When the police came, I was the only person on the scene of the crime who wasn't hurt, so I became the number one suspect. As soon as I pull up to the hospital, the detectives came and hauled my ass off to jail because they had found my gun back at the house. I had to go through a whole bunch of bullshit just to prove that the gun was registered in my name, but it wasn't the gun used for the murder. They let me go, but I got a feeling that this shit ain't over. That white man is too damn pressed, and it seems like he has his mind made up that I'm the killer. He is in the damn way!"

By the time I got finished telling Ty the story, her eyes were the size of quarters. "Damn, girl, I'm sorry you had to go through all that. For the first time in life I'm at a loss for words. Tiana and Ma Dukes…are they okay?"

"I don't know what's going on, but I need to hurry up and get to this hospital and find out."

"Did you see the person who killed your dad?"

"Nah. He had on all black, and he left just as fast as he came. I don't know who it was, but he was right on time," I lied. I loved Ty, but I knew that she loved to gossip. I didn't want the news that Chief had killed my dad floating around the hood. Chief had saved our asses, so I wasn't about to snitch on him. But that didn't change the fact that I still despised him for what he had done to my mama.

"Well, I'm just glad that y'all are good. Don't worry about Tiana. I know she is going to pull through. I love y'all like my own family. But damn, bitch, I didn't know you were around here toting guns and shit!"

"Yeah, well, it's a lot of shit you don't know," I mumbled.

Ty was still talking, but my mind had drifted off to Tiana and my mom. I prayed to God that my sister made it out of that hospital alive, and that my mother could keep hold of her sanity after everything she had been through.

When we finally pulled up to the emergency room entrance, I noticed that my car was no longer there. "I don't have time for this bullshit, man! Somebody is about to have to pay for this." I was so irked with the events of the day. I needed a blunt full of loud and a stiff drink to calm my nerves.

"Don't worry about that, boo. Go up there and check on your family. I'll find out what's going on with this car situation and then I'll be up," Ty said.

"Thank you so much, girl."

"You ain't gotta thank me. Now bye!"

I practically jumped out of the car and ran through the hospital doors. I was disgusted with the people who were in there hacking and not covering their mouths and blowing their noses all loud right in the middle of the waiting room.

"Can I help you, ma'am?" the lady behind the desk asked.

"Yes. I'm trying to find out where Tiana Gellar is. I'm her sister."

"Okay, give me one moment." The lady started typing on her computer. "Tiana Gellar is in the ICU. I can have someone take you right to her if you'd like."

The lady got one of the nurses to escort me to ICU, and it felt like time stood still on the way up there. Before I realized it, tears were flowing down my face uncontrollably. The fear of the unknown was overwhelming. I said a silent prayer before I walked off.

As soon as I stepped off the elevator and into the ICU waiting room, I spotted my mom and Aunt Precious. I noticed that they both had somber looks on their faces. That alone made my heart sink into my stomach.

I gave both of them a hug and a kiss on the cheek before I started asking questions. "What's going on with Tiana? What did the doctors say? Is she going to be alright?"

"Take a deep breath, London and calm your nerves, baby. Everything is going to be fine," Aunt Precious said.

"I'll feel a whole lot better once I know what's going on with my sister. So could someone please fill me in?" I snapped, getting irritated. I didn't mean any disrespect, but it was not the time for anyone to be telling me to calm down when my sister was laid up in the hospital.

"Tiana is fine honey," my mom cut in when she picked up on my attitude. "Right now we are just waiting for the doctor to let us know when she makes it out of surgery. She was shot in the back and the bullet pierced her left kidney. It was severely damaged beyond repair. The doctor had to remove it because of the excessive internal bleeding and he wanted to prevent the toxins from spreading to other organs. They are going to put her on antibiotics to treat any infections she may have. Other than that, your sister will be back to normal in no time. She might be in pain for a while, but the worst part is over."

A sigh of relief escaped my lips, and I felt a weight lifted off my shoulders. I knew that you could live a normal life with just one kidney. "Thank God! How long has she been in surgery?"

My mom looked at the clock on her phone. "A little over two hours," she answered.

"I guess we have a couple of hours to kill. Have you been examined by a doctor?"

She looked at me like I was crazy. "Why would *I* get examined by a doctor when my daughter was the one who was shot? Tiana needs me and I'm not leaving this waiting room until I know for a fact that she is in the clear!"

"I tried to tell her stubborn ass to at least let a doctor do a quick exam," Aunt Precious intervened. "You may think nothing is wrong with *you*, but you have another life to worry about other than your own. Your baby has been put under a lot of stress, and that alone can cause issues."

"I said I'm all right!" she got up and stormed off toward the bathroom.

Aunt Precious had a stunned look on her face, and I would bet my last dollar that 'Was it something I said?' was going through her mind at that moment. I asked her if she could give me a moment to go check on my mom, and she just gave me a head nod. I went in the ladies' room and found my mom standing in front of the mirror sobbing heavily.

"All this is my fault! My baby girl just got shot because of *me*! She didn't deserve any of this. That bullet was meant for me," she cried. It was hard to make out what she else she said because she was crying so hard.

I put my arms around her and pulled her close to me, which was kind of hard with her belly being the size of a basketball. "It's not your fault. Don't blame and beat yourself up behind something that was out of your control. You're fine. Tiana's going to be fine. It's time for us to put all of this behind us and move on with our lives. The best part about it is you no longer have to live your life in fear and looking over your shoulder. The big scary monster is gone."

My last statement got her to crack a slight smile. "I guess you're right, London. I'll be glad when I have this little boy. These pregnancy hormones are a bitch! Just in the past seven and a half months I have cried enough tears for a lifetime."

Even though she wore her troubles on her face, my mom was still a beautiful woman. She had been through so much in her life, but I knew that she was going to bounce back. I had always known her to be strong and resilient. There was nothing that she couldn't overcome.

My mom was still looking in the mirror, running her fingers through her short hair. "Girl I need to get this hair fixed ASAP. Let's go see if the doctor came out yet." She forced a smile on her face, and we walked back into the waiting room.

"Is everything okay?" a concerned Aunt Precious asked.

"I'm good, girl. I have a lot on my plate right now, but I'll be fine."

"Has anybody heard from Milan?" I asked. Even with all the bad blood, I still thought she would want to know if Tiana was going to be okay or not. She is still her sister after all.

"I haven't heard from her, but I have tried to reach out to her and let her know what happened to Tiana. She didn't return my call, and I ain't about to chase that heifer. I left her a message and told her what was going on. So as far as I'm concerned, my job is done," my mom said.

"I tried to call her too and I sent her a text message. I didn't get a response either," I added.

"Well, we aren't going to beg her to be by her sister's side. Anybody with any type of love in their heart would have been here. I'm too through with Milan!" my mom waved her hand dismissively.

"Which one of you is the mother of Tiana Gellar?" the doctor interrupted. He was either too young to be a doctor or he looked damn good for his age.

"I'm her mother, Silina Smith," she reached out and shook his hand.

"Tiana has successfully made it out of surgery, and we have put her in recovery. She is still sedated, and we are administering her antibiotics through an IV for any potential infection. We're going to keep her here for the next couple of days just to keep an eye on her. Luckily, the bullet went straight through her kidney only and didn't damage any of her other internal organs. Tiana is very blessed. Now she'll be in a lot of pain for a while, but she should be back to normal within six weeks. It could be sooner or it could be later of course. It depends on her strength and stamina. We will give you more information about what to do at home when she is closer to her discharge day. If you want, you all can go and see her."

"Thank you so much, doctor. Thank you and the rest of the medical team that saved my baby."

"Don't thank me, thank *God*." He smiled and motioned for us to follow him to Tiana's room.

Tiana was in what appeared to be a deep, peaceful sleep when we walked in the room. I went and sat right beside her on the bed and grabbed her hand. My mom sat in the chair next to it. Aunt Precious stood up on the opposite side of the bed as my mom.

I leaned down kissed Tiana all over her face. I wanted to hug her, but I was too scared I would hurt her. "I'm so glad that my sister is going to be okay!"

"What did you think? I was gonna die? Even a bullet can't stop me," Tiana said in a weak and gravelly voice as her eyes fluttered and tried to adjust to the bright lights in the room.

CHAPTER TWO
Silina

All of the joy and excitement was quickly drained out of the hospital room when Chief walked in. He must have thought that shit was sweet since he came to our rescue, but it wasn't. If anything, I was wondering how the fuck he'd just so happened to show up at the right time. I hadn't seen or heard from him since Tiana shot him, so I didn't know what to expect. Tiana was looking him right in his eyes with an evil glare on her face.

Precious was the first one to speak. "Oh hell no! What the fuck is this trifling ass nigga doing in here?"

"I'm here to check on my family. What do you think?"

"*Your* family? Nigga please! This is no longer your family. Silina doesn't want you anywhere near her," Aunt Precious said.

"Neither do I," Tiana spoke.

"You know what that means. You need to get the fuck out!" Precious told him.

"And if I don't, then what?" Chief smirked.

Precious got up and stood in his face, and it looked like a midget standing toe to toe with a giant because she was so short. She was shaped like a midget too with big titties and a huge butt. "Then shit is gonna get real ugly up in this hospital," she said through clenched teeth.

Chief laughed her off like she was a joke. "From where I'm standing, shit is already ugly up in this bitch. Now get the fuck out of my face before you see *me* get ugly."

Precious stepped even closer to him and before anyone even saw it coming she punched Chief square in the face. She hit him so hard that his head turned. Within seconds he clenched his huge hands around Precious' throat.

"Oh hell nah!" I jumped up out of my chair to defend my friend, and London was right behind me.

Tiana was in her bed watching the drama unfold, looking like she wished she had a part in it. "Get him the fuck out of here!"

Had I not been in the process of trying to take it to Chief's ass for touching my best friend I would have laid Tiana out for talking like that in front of me. They knew I didn't play that shit. As soon as I got close to Chief a sharp pain ripped through my abdomen, causing me to double over in pain. Chief let go of Precious, who fell to the ground like a sack of potatoes, and tried to come to my aid.

"What's wrong Silina?" he asked with concern in his voice. He tried to put his arms around me, but I slapped the taste out of his mouth. Everything about him still disgusted me, and I didn't want him anywhere near me.

I heard London, Tiana, and Precious asking me if I was all right; my pain wouldn't allow me to answer them. I waddled back over to the chair and sat down. I watched Tiana page the nurse from the phone that was in her room. Chief was standing there looking like he didn't know what to do next, and Precious was trying to pick herself up off the floor and catch her breathe at the same time. Not even two minutes later, I felt a warm gush of liquid start flowing down my legs.

"Silina, you're water just broke!" Precious shouted. I looked at her like, 'No, really, bitch?'

A nurse walked in the room and asked what the problem was, and she quickly got her answer when she saw me bent over in the chair with a puddle between my legs. She rushed out of the room just as quickly as she'd come in. The next time she came in, she had a wheelchair with her. By this time I was ready to ball up in a fetal position on the floor. The contractions I was having were so agonizing that I couldn't focus on anything else. It felt like somebody was stabbing me in my uterus.

Even though I tried to resist, Chief helped lift me into the wheelchair. "You might as well put all the bullshit to the side because if you're about to have my baby, I'm not going anywhere," he whispered.

"Call me, Mama. I'll be right here. I'm not going anywhere," Tiana said and smiled.

London stopped the nurse before she wheeled me out of the room and put her hands on my belly and kissed me on the cheek. "I'll be right here too, Mama. I'm gonna stay with Tiana. Keep us updated please, Aunt Precious."

"I will." She shot Chief a nasty look.

I was finally taken out of the room and to the maternity ward. The nurse wheeled me to labor and delivery with Chief and Precious right behind us. With both of them about to be in the delivery room with me, I knew that the drama was far from over.

"I can't be in labor, P. It's too early. I'm only 31 weeks!" I said to Precious while she was in the bathroom helping me get into the hospital gown the nurse had given me.

The kind woman must have heard my concern because she spoke before Precious could even get a word out. "We're going to do everything we can to ensure that you have a safe delivery. We deliver premature babies every day. Some mothers are in earlier stages of their pregnancy than you are. Yet most of our parents leave with a healthy, happy baby. We have an awesome team on standby in our NICU. They're some of the best in the country. No need to worry mommy to be!"

"Aaaggghhh!" At that moment another contraction ripped through my uterus. I crouched down on the floor in the bathroom and balled up in a knot to try to alleviate some of the pain. Precious was rubbing my back and trying her best to comfort me.

Once the contraction subsided, we walked out of the bathroom and the nurse got me situated on the bed and hooked up to the fetal monitor. Chief was sitting in the room chilling like he was right. The mere sight of him pissed me off. I really didn't want him anywhere near me, but I wasn't going to deny him the right of seeing his first child come into the world. I could feel the tension between him and Precious, and I knew that the only reason she was keeping her cool was off the strength of me and her god son.

An hour and a half passed and my contractions were coming three minutes apart and getting more agonizing by the second. "Somebody, get me some drugs please! I can't take this shit!"

Chief tried his hand once again. He came and stood beside me and rubbed my stomach. I looked at that motherfucker like he had grown another head and snatched his hand off my stomach like it was on fire. "Let's make something clear right here and right now. I don't want you touching me *at all*! I really don't even want you to breathe the same air as me. And I damn sure don't want to look at you. Be glad that I'm allowing you to watch the birth of your child, and let's just leave it at that. Next time you try to touch me, your arm is going to come back without a hand attached. Don't fuck with me, Chief! Go sit over there in your corner and leave me the hell alone!"

He threw his hands up in surrender and said, "I was only trying to comfort you! That's all. No need to be a bitch about it."

Before I could let him have it, a doctor walked into the room and told me she was going to check my cervix. The discomfort of her three fingers entering my cervix and pressing down on my uterus combined with the painful contraction made me to want to kick the doctor in her face.

"It looks like you're going to have to deliver naturally. It's a little too late for an epidural. You're eight and a half centimeters dilated, and at that rate, you'll be pushing any minute!"

I didn't even have time to think about the fact that I actually had to push out a baby with no type of medication because another contraction came. This time I felt a lot of pressure like my vagina was being split apart. "Aaaggghhh!" I squeezed Precious' hand so hard that I thought I felt her bones crushing.

The doctor and nurses were scrambling around the room, getting everything in place to deliver the baby. One of the nurses came and removed the bottom of my bed then put a small stool for the doctor to sit on. The doctor told Chief and

Precious to hold my legs and she came and sat on the stool. Her face was right between my legs, and she used her fingers to open me up and look inside.

"The head is coming down, Silina. On your next contraction I need you to push as hard as you can!"

The contraction came thirty seconds later, and I curled my back around my belly and pushed as hard as I could. It felt like my vagina was on fire when a little head full of black curls appeared. I could see everything going on through the mirror that one of the nurses was holding up.

The doctor took the nose bulb on her table and cleared the baby's nasal passage. "Okay, Silina, one more push, give it all you've got!"

I pushed with everything in me and my baby slid out. The doctor held him up to my face and our eyes met for the first time. I fell in love with my beautiful baby boy at first sight.

"He's so adorable!" Precious squealed.

He was so small that I was afraid if I held him I might break him. He didn't have any color yet, but I could tell by his ears that he was going to have skin the color of honey like me and his sisters. Chief's eyes lit up like a Christmas tree when he laid eyes on him, showing nothing but pure joy. The doctor handed Chief the scissors and while he was cutting the umbilical cord my placenta came out.

"Waaahhh, waaahhh!" wails from my baby boy filled the room right after the cord was cut. The nurse immediately put him on the scale and the numbers read 3lbs and 4oz. She then wrapped him up, put him in the incubator and rolled him out of the room.

"Wait a minute, where's she going with my baby? I didn't even get a chance to hold him!"

"I'm sorry, Silina, but your son was born prematurely, so we can't waste any time getting him to the NICU. There will be plenty of time for hugs and kisses after we make sure that you have a healthy baby boy," the doctor explained.

"Can I go with him?" Chief asked.

"I'm afraid not. Once they are done running tests in the NICU, you will be able to go see him in the nursery."

Chief looked like a piece of his heart and soul had been snatched away from him. I could see the genuine love he had for his son. The way he looked at him the moment he was born let me know that it was love at first sight. I even caught him shedding a tear even though I knew he would never admit it.

I prayed for my son's health and I left it in God's hands. I wasn't worried because I knew that my baby boy was going to be strong and healthy.

"What are you going to name my god baby?" Precious, who was now sitting in a chair, asked. Her titties were sitting on top of the table she was behind and her ass was spilling all over the sides of the chair. Her natural twist out had turned into an afro.

"I'm going to name him Jordan," I finally answered, not even caring to hear Chief's opinion.

"I think I like the sound of that," he smiled.

"Yeah, well who the fuck asked you?" Precious asked him.

Chief looked at me like he was trying not to flip a lid. "Can we get a private moment without your lil sidekick here? We have important shit that needs to be discussed, and it ain't any of her damn business," Chief said.

"You're right. We do need to discuss a few things. Precious, could you give us a moment please?"

"Don't let that bitch ass nigga sweet talk you, girl. Don't forget what a low down dirty dog he really is!" Precious got up and left the room, letting the door slam behind her.

"I thought that bitch would never fucking leave!" Chief stated.

"If I were you I would stop using that bitch word so loosely. I ain't pregnant no more, so don't fuck with me. This is how this discussion is going to go. I'm going to talk, and you're going to listen. First things first, since you want to be popping up out of the woodworks after several months, you need to get ready to sign these divorce papers. I don't want to have your last name for another minute. So the sooner we can get this done, the better it'll be for me."

"Damn! You're throwing a divorce in a nigga's face already? I know what I did was wrong but—"

"Save it!" I put my hand up in front of his face to stop anymore words from coming out of his mouth. "I'm not trying to hear none of your bullshit excuses, and you can take your worthless apologies and shove them up you're fuckin' ass. I'm telling you right now that you're wasting your time trying to explain anything to me because I ain't trying to hear it."

"This is a marriage, Silina. You always said you wanted us to grow old together. You think them old happy couples that you love so much haven't been through shit in their marriage?"

"I doubt that any of the shit they've been through involved their husbands fucking their daughters!"

"Shit, you'd be surprised about what goes on behind closed doors," Chief mumbled. "We can't just throw away our marriage and everything that we've built together. You just had my son, and he deserves a family."

"Well, you threw all that away when you hopped in between the sheets with my daughter. Just because I had a son by you, it doesn't mean we have to be together. For the rest of the days I have left here on this earth, I am going to be happy. That can't happen with you, so I have to cut you off, boo."

"Damn! So it's over like that, huh? I just saved you and your daughters' lives and you want to leave me already. You don't even want to try to work this out?"

"So you think because you saved my life I owe you? I don't owe you shit! You're the one that ruined this marriage, not me! So don't come with that bullshit. I can't believe you tried to play that card. You got to be a damn fool to think that I would consider staying married to you after what you did. You ain't nothing but a hoe ass nigga!"

"You got it for now, Silina. Get used to seeing my face, though. Because as long as my son is in this hospital, I ain't leaving." Chief sat in the recliner for overnight guests and kicked his feet up. "And after he leaves the hospital, you'll still be seeing a lot of me." He looked up at me and smirked like he was satisfied that he was getting under my skin.

This is going to be a long 18 years.

CHAPTER THREE
Elijah

It was hot as hell when I stepped out of the airport in St. Lucia. July was the hottest month on the island, and my black ass didn't mix well with heat. The dark gray sky looked like it was about to fall as I stood on the curb waiting for my ride. I heard thunder clap, and seconds later a bolt of lightning lit up the sky. The clouds opened up, and the rain started to pour heavily. A black Ashton Martin pulled up to the curb, and after I got in, the driver sped off.

The storm only lasted for about five minutes, and then the sun reappeared. Looking at the scenery and how peaceful and beautiful the island was made me think about my lady, Milan. I wished she was in St. Lucia with me, but I wasn't there for leisure. It was all about business.

My Columbian connect, Diego, called me and told me to come see him ASAP. I knew that it had to be something serious for him to call me all the way out in the Caribbean, so I hopped on a plane within hours. I was directly plugged in with a Columbian cartel and I got pure cocaine sent to me straight from the coca fields. I got the shit for dirt cheap and sold it for whatever price I wanted to because I knew that niggas would pay for it. The shit I was pushing was more potent than the competition, and I sold it for less. It didn't matter to me because I was profiting anywhere from $25,000 to $30,000 off each brick.

We entered the tall white gate and went down the long winding driveway that led to Diego's villa, which sat on the beach. When I got out of the car and rung the doorbell, I was greeted by a sexy Hispanic lady.

"Aye, papi, Diego no tell me you so handsome." The young lady flirted in her thick Spanish accent. She had long, thick black hair that hung down to her plump ass. She had pretty brown eyes and full lips, and her skin was a caramel tone. The only thing she had on was a black bikini. My dick jumped as I thought about how many different positions I could twist her little ass up in. I knew I had a woman, but I was still a man, and looking ain't never hurt nobody.

"Don't just stand there. Follow me." She walked seductively through the house leading me to the deck in the back of the house that faced the beach.

Diego caught me watching her walk away and said, "That's a sexy bitch aye? That fine piece of ass cost me a lot of pesos. I can let you sample the candy for just a small amount." He nudged me with his elbow and laughed at his damn self.

"I'm good on that for now." I laughed with him.

"Que pasa, Elijah? It's good to see you. Come have a seat and take a drink with me." We went and sat on the beach chairs, and he poured us shots of d'usse cognac. We threw the shots back. As soon as I put my cup down, Diego refilled my glass.

"So what's up, man? I know you didn't call me out here for a social visit."

Diego looked at me and chuckled. "It's always straight to business with you, no time to shoot the shit!"

"You got that right. I wouldn't have it any other way. Too many motherfuckers are waiting for me to slip up. The first time I put business to the side for anything else will be the first time a nigga could catch me slipping."

"Si, si, well let's get down to business. I called you all the way out here because I have some important information that can't be discussed over phones."

"Well, stop beating around the bush and let me know something!" I was getting impatient by then. Everyone was afraid of Diego because he was known for making motherfuckers disappear, but not me. I didn't fear a thing but God, especially not a man that could bleed just like I could.

"You know you remind me a lot of your father. Well respected and feared out in the streets but also smart enough to keep your money clean. You are very wise for such a young age. Your father was one of my best friends, and I promised him that if anything ever happened to him I would watch over you. When he was killed, I made a promise to myself that I would find out who was behind it and wipe out every single person in their bloodline."

The mention of my father and his murder caused my ears to perk up. Diego had to know something about it for him to bring it up. I had never heard Diego even speak of my father's murder up until then.

"What do you know, Diego?"

He pulled an envelope from underneath his chair. "After all these years, I finally found out who orchestrated your father's murder. I thought long and hard on this and I know that you want your father's killer to die by your hands."

I couldn't take anymore of Diego's games. He didn't even know that he was playing with my emotions. Losing my father was the biggest tragedy of my life. My mama running off and leaving me to be with another man didn't even hurt me that bad. My father was all I knew, and he was all I had, and I was going to avenge his death if it killed me. I snatched the envelope out of his hands and ripped it open. When I saw the picture inside my blood started boiling. I crumbled the photo and envelope up and my trigger finger started itching.

"The only thing I will tell you to do is play it smart. Don't let your emotions get the best of you and put you in a sticky situation. Make your next move your best move because if you don't, you will start a war."

"You should know better than anyone that I always finish what I start," I got up and left Diego sitting there.

When I got back in the black Ashton Martin and was headed back toward the airport I was fuming. I knew that what Diego had said was right though, I had to be smart about the situation. The same nigga that had killed my dad had already caught me slipping once, and I damn sure wasn't about to let it happen again.

The more I thought about it, the clearer shit became to me. I didn't even need to ask Diego any questions because I had already put everything together myself. The same nigga that was gunning for me, trying to take over my streets, had taken my pops out the game for that exact same reason. That motherfucker was on a power trip that was about to come to an end.

Damn, I can't believe that Chief is the one that had my pops killed!

London

My mother and Tiana were both due to be released from the hospital on the same day. I had stayed there with them for four days, and I couldn't wait to get home. I left a couple of hours before them so I could clean the house and cook them a meal.

When I pulled up to the house, a gloomy feeling came over me. The first thing I noticed was the yellow tape that was scattered all over our front yard. When I walked into the house, the putrid smell of old blood filled my nostrils and damn near suffocated me. Going into the kitchen and seeing the floor covered in blood, Tiana's and our dad's, made me get sick to my stomach. I wasted no time pulling out the bleach, Fabuloso, and Oxy Clean. I poured so many chemicals on the floor that I had to open every window in the house just to get some ventilation. I blasted my Trey Songz CD and got to work.

Two and a half hours later I had deep cleaned the house from top to bottom, lit candles in every room, and started on dinner. I decided to make baked spaghetti, garlic bread, and a Caesar salad. After everything was complete, I jumped in the shower. Before Tiana and my mom made it home I stuck a towel under my door and lit up one of my pre-rolled blunts. I also lit an incense in my room to mask the smell of the loud I was blowing. I knew my mom would kill me if she knew I was smoking in her house.

I had almost smoked myself to sleep when my phone rang and the name Elijah popped up on my screen.

"Hey, sexy. What's up?" I answered.

"What's good baby, girl? I'm on my way to Virginia right now. I wanted to see if you could meet me a little later on tonight. I got something I need to holla at you about."

"My mom and sister are on their way home from the hospital. But once I make sure they're straight, I can meet up with you. How does nine o'clock sound?"

"Both your mom and sister were in the hospital? Damn! Milan, I didn't know that. As far as I knew, you didn't have any family."

"Yeah, well we may have our differences, but if they need me, I'm going to be there."

"True. I feel you on that. I gotta go, but call me if anything changes."

He hung up without even giving me a chance to say another word. I was definitely going to meet up with him, but I couldn't keep up the charade of being Milan. Being a liar and deceiver wasn't me, so I decided that I was going to tell him the truth. The doorbell rang continuously and snapped me out of my thoughts. I knew it was Tiana because she would always keep her finger on the doorbell until someone answered the door.

I unlocked it, and before I could turn the knob all the way, Tiana was bum rushing the door. "It smells good up in here. What you in here cooking up? Lord knows I'm starving."

Tiana didn't even wait for an answer. She just walked straight into the kitchen. My mom entered the house behind her, but she didn't come with my baby brother, Jordan. He had to stay in the hospital just a little while longer until he gained more weight because of his premature birth. My mom looked around, and I could tell she was impressed by how clean the house was.

"Wow! It looks good in here London. Let's go eat that delicious smelling meal you've cooked."

I followed my mom into the dining room. Tiana was already bringing the food to the table. While she finished bringing it out, I went and grabbed plates, cups, and silverware. We all sat down, blessed our food, and dug in.

"Uh uhn, mama, London is trying to make us sick with this raw hamburger meat she served us." Tiana cracked a smile.

"Whatever, heifer, I see you ain't stopped chewing to take a breath." I laughed.

There was a moment of silence, and it was kind of uncomfortable. We were all trying to adjust to being back in the very place that tragedy had struck. I watched Tiana constantly look around like someone was going to pop out and get her, but I couldn't blame her for that. My mom looked like she was at a loss for words.

Tiana was the first to break the silence. "What's up with Chief? Have you been talking to him behind our back mama?"

My mom looked like she wanted to slap the shit out of Tiana. Instead she said, "I'm a grown ass woman, I don't have to do shit behind anybody's back. Let's not forget who the parent is in this situation. You don't question me about a damn thing I do!"

"Sorry, Ma. I was just saying. I find it funny that Chief would go out of his way to try to save someone that shot him. I mean he came right in the knick of time too. It's almost like he was watching us."

"Knowing Chief, he probably was watching us or had somebody else watching. My guess is as good as yours. I'm glad he did come when he did, but that doesn't mean I'm going to welcome him back with open arms."

"I don't trust him at all. I know that nigga got ulterior motives."

My mom cut her eyes at Tiana and gave her one of those 'keep trying me' looks. I knew that she didn't tolerate any form of disrespect and using that type of language around her was one. I couldn't say that I didn't agree with Tiana though, because I didn't trust Chief either. I didn't know what he had up his sleeve, but something just didn't sit right with me.

"Nobody is gonna fuck with this family anymore. I'll kill Chief myself before I let anybody put my kids in harms way again." By the look in my mom's eyes and the seriousness in her tone, I knew that she meant every word. "Now that that's over, I'm about to go take a shower and go shopping. Anybody wanna come with?" she asked as she was leaving from the table.

"I do. Are you treating?" Tiana joked as she got up and started clearing the table.

"Don't you need to be getting some rest and relaxation?" I asked. I didn't want her to start moving too fast only a few days after surgery.

"Girl, please! I couldn't do nothing but rest and relax for five days straight in a hospital bed. I'm getting out of this house. I ain't about to lay in the bed and be miserable."

I couldn't do anything but smile. My sister was back like nothing had ever happened to her. She never let anything get the best of her, and I admired her for that.

"The doctor gave you a medical leave of absence, officially excusing you from school for six weeks. I bet you follow that order, though!" I teased.

"You damn right I'm gonna follow that order. A six-week break from school…chile please! You know I won't be entering any classrooms until then."

We both laughed, but I knew she wasn't playing.

"I'll catch y'all later. I need to get ready for my date," I said.

"Who're you going on a date with, girl? When did this happen?" Tiana was all in my business.

"Don't worry about it, nosy." I smirked, knowing that she was going to keep asking until she got an answer.

She walked over to me and pinched the skin on my arm. "You better start talking!"

I pinched the skin on her hand to make her let me go. "Get off me, trick! I'll tell you about it when I get back. I got shit to do. Bye!" I ran off before she could protest.

I went to my room and started pulling stuff out of my closet and drawers to find something to wear. I needed to know where we were going so I could know how to dress. So I sent Elijah a text message, asking where we were meeting. He responded and told me to meet him at the Ocean Front.

I knew that the Ocean Front meant walking, so that counted out any outfit that required heels. I settled for a black and white sundress that dipped down to my lower back with a pair of black sandals. I flat ironed my weave bone straight with a part down the middle. I sprayed on one of my favorite scents, Pink Friday by Nicki Minaj. The only makeup I applied was some eyeliner, lip gloss, and a drop of concealer to hide my beauty mark on my nose. I glued some lash strips on my eyelids. After that, I was satisfied with my look.

I gave myself the once over in my full-length mirror, and I loved the way the dress was hugging my curves. I had been putting on weight over the past few months, and it definitely showed in all the right places. My hips and thighs were thicker than they had ever been.

I looked at the time and it was nine o'clock on the dot. I planned to be late anyway, but I knew it took twenty minutes to get down the beach, so I left. I got in my car, blasted my Yo Gotti CD, and was out. I got there in about fifteen minutes instead of twenty and I parked my car in the 17th Street parking area. I called Elijah to find out exactly where he was.

"Hello," he answered. His voice was so deep and sexy that just hearing it gave me butterflies.

"Hey, I'm down here parked on 17th and Atlantic, where you?"

"I'm parked on the same street. Just walk to the front of the parking lot like you're about to cross the street, and I'm gonna be standing right there."

"A'ight. Cool." I hung up.

I walked to the front and he was standing right where he'd said he would be. It was dark outside, but it was like a light was shining down on his fine ass. He was wearing a wife beater, so I could see every muscle in his arms, shoulders, and chest rippling. I could even see the imprint of his eight pack through the beater. He had on some white destroyed denim shorts and some white Polo flip flops. I was enjoying all 6'3" of that eye candy while trying to think of a new way to please him.

"About time yo ass got down here. I was starting to think you were gonna stand a nigga up." He wrapped his arm around my waist and pulled me close to him so we were walking side by side.

"Now why would I do something like that?" I batted my lashes.

"I don't know, but you look good as hell right now. I see that phat ass jigglin' in that dress." He grabbed a handful of my juicy ass as we were crossing the street.

I was laughing and giggling, enjoying every minute of it. It was crazy how I didn't even know him, but he made me feel good. I was sure that feeling was going to come to an end once I told him I wasn't Milan.

We walked until we reached the sand. Elijah took his flip flops off and told me to join him. I took my sandals off, and we walked through the sand until we got closer to the water. The bright lights from all of the hotels and other businesses on the strip mixed with the waves crashing and the cool breeze created a beautiful scene. The moon was full, and it looked like it was so close that you could reach out and grab it. Elijah intertwined his fingers with mine and we walked further down the beach until we got to a spot where a man was standing.

"Thanks for watching my stuff. Here you go." Elijah handed him a hundred dollar bill.

Damn! He must be balling just giving away a hundred dollars like that.

We walked a few more feet and what I saw would have swept any girl off her feet. Elijah had set up a little picnic on the beach. There was a large red blanket laid out on the sand with a picnic basket sitting on top of it. A small black radio was playing slow jams and there were two wineglasses and a cooler. Elijah guided me to the blanket and I sat down. He opened the picnic basket and the first thing he pulled out was a dozen white roses.

"These are beautiful. Thank you."

"Beautiful flowers for a beautiful lady. I brought some bread and shit in case you were hungry. I brought fresh assorted cold cuts from a Jewish deli too. We can make sandwiches. No need to eat fancy on the sand right?" He said, flashing that irresistible smile.

I laughed and answered, "Sounds good to me. Look, before we go any further with this evening I have something I need to tell you."

By the change in his expression, I could already tell he was expecting the worst. "The last time I heard that it wasn't good news. So what's up? What you need to tell me?"

I paused for a moment and took a deep breath. It was then that I realized how wrong I was about the entire situation. In the process of trying to get back at Milan, I hadn't considered anyone else's feelings.

"Don't beat around the bush with me. Just spit it out," he said after a moment of silence.

I just said fuck it to myself and told him exactly what it was. "It ain't no easy way to put this, but I wanted to tell you that I'm not Milan."

"You ain't Milan? What the fuck do you mean you ain't Milan? What you're saying ain't making no sense to me right now so I'ma need you to elaborate."

"I'm Milan's twin sister, *London*. When you found me trying to get into her place, I was there because I thought she was working with our step dad to try and sabotage our family.

So I wanted to pay her a visit. When I saw that you thought I was her, I used that as an opportunity to get back at her."

Elijah looked like a light bulb had just gone off in his head. "Why would you think she was trying to work with your step dad to try and sabotage your family? From what she told me, *y'all* were the fucked up ones."

"*Us?* Yeah, I know that Milan has fed you a whole lot of bullshit and lies. That's what she does. *She's* the fucked up one. I was trying to get back at her for fucking her mama's husband. We cut her ass off, not the other way around. I don't know what Milan told you, but whatever it was, I'm sure it was all false info. That girl can't be trusted."

"Well, how do I know that *you* can be trusted? Why should I take your word and believe that Milan has been lying to me the whole time?" he questioned.

"You don't have to. I did my job by coming here and telling you the truth." I started to get up so I could leave.

"Hold on, shorty. I ain't saying that I don't believe you. I respect you for being a woman and keeping it real with a nigga. I didn't know shit like this happened in real life. Had I known Milan had a twin, I probably would have tried to get with both of y'all," he cracked a smile.

I couldn't help but smile back because even after what I had just told him, he was still able to crack jokes with me.

"Hmph, that will never happen," I laughed.

"On the real, though…what type of shit is Milan really on? You mean to tell me that she was actually sleeping with her step pops?"

"She was actually sleeping with the nigga! For two years at that, and then she had the nerve to throw it in my mama's face. I don't even know how they hid it for so long, but that's some foul shit. I watched my mom go through a lot of emotions behind that. I had to do something to make her feel the same pain that she had made my mama go through," I explained.

"I feel you on that. I believe that everything happens for a reason. I would have been in the blind about who Milan really was if you hadn't done what you did and made the decision to come clean about it."

"You don't even know the half of it. Milan's a hot mess. Anyway, that's the reason that I came down here to meet you. I wanted to confess to you face to face. I apologize about dragging you into our family drama and wasting your time. Just so you know, you have all the elements for a very romantic evening. Keep that in mind the next time you want to flatter a special lady." I winked at him.

"You might as well sit down and enjoy these sandwiches and red berry Ciroc with me. You came all the way down here. Ain't no need for either one of us to waste a trip."

With that said I sat back down on the blanket and poured myself a drink. Elijah was right. I might as well enjoy the rest of our night—possibly our last—together.

"So tell me about yourself London. I'm sitting here sharing a romantic evening with a stranger," he laughed.

"What do you want to know?" I replied bashfully.

"What do you do?" he asked.

"I sell drugs," I replied nonchalantly.

He looked at me like I was crazy and I couldn't do anything but laugh.

"Legally that is. I have a Bachelor's degree in Pharmaceutical Sales and right now I'm back in school working on my masters in Pharmacology. Once I'm finished with that I'm going back for my doctorate. So technically, I have a career in selling drugs. I wish I had a camera to show you how your face dropped when I said I sold drugs," I busted out laughing again.

"That shit just caught me off guard. I ain't used to women saying that they sell drugs and if they do I advise them not to. But it sounds like you have a lot going for yourself, that's what's up."

"What about you? What do you do?"

"We'll get into that later. Right now I want to know everything about you. Has your relationship with your sister always been rocky?"

"Not when we were kids. We were inseparable back then. Nobody could ever fuck with one of us without fucking with the other. We used to dress alike and everything. We even played tricks on people who didn't know us and switch places. I was always the smart one so I would go to her classes for her on days that she had tests and take them for her so she would pass. Once we got in the eighth grade that's when everything changed. For some reason it seemed like there was some type of competition between us. People always talked about how smart I was and how far I was going to get and she hated that. She started acting funny towards me and our family but nobody ever knew why. By the time we got in high school it was like we were complete strangers. She went her way and I went mine. I'll never forget the day that I whipped a girl's ass for calling my sister a hoe and trying to put her on blast. Four of her friends jumped in the fight and Milan stood right there and watched. She didn't lift a finger. After some of my friend's saw what was going on they jumped in to help me and I stopped fighting to whip Milan's ass. Shit was never the same between us after that day. I can't lie that shit hurt me to the core," I confessed.

"Damn that's fucked up," he shook his head in disbelief and there was a moment of silence.

He broke he silence by asking me, "So how do you think your man would feel if he knew what we did?"

"That question would deserve an answer if I had a man, but I don't so I don't know how he would feel."

"It's hard to believe that someone as beautiful as you doesn't have a man," he gazed into my eyes and the words he spoke along with the way he was looking at me made me feel all giddy inside.

"Well believe it. I haven't had a man since my junior year in college. I found out that he was cheating on me so I left his ass. My high school sweetheart did the same thing to me after a four year relationship. So after it happened for the second time I decided to just write men off for a while and focus on getting my life together for me."

I was so comfortable with him that I found myself telling him shit about myself and I didn't even know him that well.

"True. I feel you on that. All men ain't the same though so you gotta let that wall down at some point," he said.

"And I will, as soon as somebody proves to me that they are worthy of that. I ain't gonna keep giving somebody my heart for them to misuse and abuse my love. That shit is emotionally draining. I can do bad by my damn self. I'd rather be alone and happy than in a relationship and miserable."

"You just need to learn how to pick 'em that's all."

"From the looks of it you need to learn how to pick 'em too," I joked.

"I usually don't even get that involved with a female. Most of them only want what I got so I was using them for what they had. I never really let anybody get that close to me because I don't trust people. My trust issues came from watching my mama up and leave my daddy, a hell of a man if I do say so myself, to be with another man. I could never allow myself to really trust a bitch after that. And I was too busy chasing money to be in a serious relationship. I don't know how your sister slid through the crack but she proved to me why all I do is fuck 'em and duck 'em. I'm getting to the point now where I want a loyal female by my side that I can build with. Bel Biv DeVoe wasn't lying when they said 'never trust a big butt and a smile' because that shit had my judgment clouded like a motherfucker," he confessed.

"I'm sorry to hear that. I rarely hear about it being the woman that leaves her family for another man. Are you and your dad still pretty close?"

When I said that he got this distant look in his eyes and I thought I saw them get glassy, like they were watering up. "My dad was my best friend. We would still be thick as thieves if he was alive. My father was murdered," he said in a barely audible tone.

"Oh my God I had no idea. I didn't mean to bring it up, I'm sorry!" I felt like shit bringing up his deceased father.

"You're good ma, you didn't know. It's no need for you to be sorry. The motherfucker that did it is going to be sorry though."

Chills went through my body when he said that because something deep within me told me that he meant it. I looked in his eyes and no longer did I see the warm-hearted gentleman that I was talking too. I was looking in the eyes of a cold blooded killer. I knew because I saw the same look in my dad's eyes when he was about to pull the trigger on my mom. I also saw that look in Chief's eyes when he blew his brains out.

"My dad was murdered too. The only difference is I don't feel a drop of sadness behind it. My dad couldn't do any wrong in my eyes when I was a little girl. I thought we had the perfect little family. That was until I got older and realized what he was doing to my mom. He abused her every day of her life that she was with him. Then he tried to kill her about a week ago. If it wasn't for Chief shooting him in his dome he would have killed us all."

"It sounds like we had a lot of fucked up shit going on in our lives but through it all we made it," he said.

We spent the next couple of hours enjoying each other's company and talking about everything under the sun. I didn't know what was happening between us, but I liked it.

CHAPTER FOUR
Elijah

Finding out that Chief was behind my father's murder and that I had fucked Milan's twin sister, London, in less than a week blew my mind. I couldn't even be mad at London for what she had done when she told me the reason behind it. What she had revealed to me had me looking at Milan funny and doubting everything she'd ever told me. That bitch had me fooled. The whole time she had me thinking that Chief was raping her and had her interstate trafficking bricks when really she was fucking that nigga willingly. She was even pregnant with the nigga's baby, but I thought it was from her being raped.

I was starting to wonder if they were in cahoots plotting against me. I must have really been slipping because I normally would have sensed some shit like that from a mile away. Another alarm went off when I realized that Milan had gone so long without trying to contact me. It was like she just up and disappeared without a care in the world. Whatever was

60

going on, I was going to get to the bottom of it, and London was going to help me.

I didn't know if I could trust her yet, but I knew I could pick her brain for information. The more she talked the more the pieces to my puzzle fit together. I figured Milan had used me to find out what she could so that she and Chief could get everything I had and take me out of the game permanently. Little did they know that it was never going to happen.

I knew that London had just as much against them as I did, so I decided I was going to keep in touch with her. I knew I could find out everything I needed to know about Chief and his whereabouts so I could put my plan into effect. I was going to get that bitch ass nigga before he got me, and if Milan got in the way she could become a casualty of war too.

"What's up boss, I'm looking at that nigga Chief right now. What you tryna do? I can do his ass right now if you want me to," my nigga Ox said.

"Bro, watch what you saying to me over these phones. Where you at?"

"I'm at Club Aqua on Newtown. The club ain't over yet and the nigga still in here parlaying and shit."

"I'm on my way. Keep your eyes on that bitch ass nigga. Don't let him out of your sight." I hung up the phone and sped to the club he was at.

I couldn't believe that motherfucker just fell in my lap that easily. I was about to kill his ass and he wouldn't even see it coming, the same way he had my dad taken out. My trigger finger was itching as I pulled up to the place that Ox said he saw Chief. I checked out the scenery and noticed that the police were out in the parking lot, so I knew I was going to have to follow Chief if I wanted to get him. I wanted him dead but not bad enough to get myself locked up.

Ox called me again and let me know that Chief was walking out of the club. From where I was parked I could see everybody who was entering and exiting the club but no one could see me. I was parked right by the exit so when Chief left the parking lot he would have to pass me. I watched Chief walk out the door and I saw Ox coming out shortly after. Chief got in his car alone and pulled off and I followed right behind him.

We came to a stop light a few miles up and I pulled up right beside him. I cocked back the .380 I had in my lap and rolled my window down. I wanted him to see who the motherfucker was that was about to leave him slumped in the middle of the road. I put my gun out the window and started busting at the truck that Chief was in.

Pow! Pow! Pow!

His passenger window shattered instantly and I saw him duck his head down to get out of my line of fire. His tires screeched as he sped through the red light, swerving while trying to get away from the hail of bullets that was coming his way. I wasn't giving up that easily. My adrenaline was rushing as I sped off behind him. I wanted him dead bad as a bitch.

Pop! Pop! Pop!

Bullets started ricocheting off my car and busted out my windshield as Chief hung out his window and started shooting back at me. I could feel the heat from a bullet that flew right past my left ear, barely missing my head and putting a hole in my headrest. I crouched down in my seat just enough so that I could see over the steering wheel. I saw him turn around to see where he was going and I used that as an opportunity to start shooting again.

I heard police sirens in the distance so I knew that I had to do something and get the fuck out of dodge. We were almost by Booker T. High School in Norfolk by that time and I knew that the boys (cops) were hot out there. At that moment it was now or never because I knew that Chief would be on his P's and Q's now that I was after him. A lot of niggas feared Chief but I didn't fear no fucking body. I was going to show him that he wasn't the only gorilla out here in these streets.

As soon as I let off two shots he stuck his arm out the window again to shoot back. The second bullet hit him in his upper arm and he ducked back inside the car. God must have been on his side because that bitch ass nigga made it over the railroad tracks just before they shut it down for a train to pass. The police sirens were getting closer and closer so I backed up and hauled ass out of there. I went down Park Avenue and hopped on the interstate at Brambleton Ave.

I heard my phone ringing and it was Ox calling.

"Yo..."

"What the fuck happened man you took off so fast I didn't know where the fuck you was at when I got in my car. I heard guns blazing though I had to make sure shit was gravy," he said, sounding concerned.

"Nigga you already know I'm good. I need you to meet me up in Richmond so I can take care of something and I'm gonna ride back to Maryland with you."

"Fa' sho' my nigga, I got you."

I knew I had to get rid of that car so I had to take it to the chop shop up in Richmond.

"Fuck! I can't believe I let this nigga get away!"

I knew that I had to play it smart that time around but the next time I came across him, I promised myself that I was going to take his ass out no matter what.

Chief

"Aaaggghhh! Shit!" I yelped out in pain.

After getting shot in my arm by that bitch ass nigga Elijah I went to this bitch named Tonya crib that I used to fuck with out in Tidewater Park. She was a hood bitch and she was most definitely a ride or die bitch. I used to fuck with her back in the day but she had too much shit with her.

Tonya smacked her lips. "Stop screaming like a little bitch! It'll be over soon."

She went back to removing the bullet that was in my arm. She had just poured some vodka in the gunshot wound and now she was digging around in the hole in my arm with a hot knife. That bullet did some damage to my shit. My damn arm busted open like one of those red hot sausages when you cook them too long. I had blood all over the inside of my whip.

"I'ma kill this nigga!" I snapped, trying to take my mind off the pain.

I should have known that it was only a matter of time before the nigga came after me for trying to kill him. So much time had gone by that I got too comfortable and got caught slipping. The next time he was going to be the getting caught and I was going to feed him to the sharks.

"I can't believe you shot at him all those times and ain't hit the nigga once! You're losing it Chief. The nigga I knew wouldn't have left until that nigga was dead. You better get it together because that nigga not playing with you. You better be careful too because you know he fuck with those Colombians. Starting a war with them ain't nothing but a death wish," Tonya warned as she finally removed the bullet from my arm.

"Fuck Elijah and those damn Colombians. I'm not worried about that shit; them motherfuckers can catch a bullet just like anybody else!"

"Well it looks like you were the one that caught a bullet tonight and he got away without a scratch," Tonya replied.

One of the things I couldn't stand about Tonya was that her ass said whatever the fuck came to her mind and didn't give a fuck. It wasn't the time for her to be popping shit and she knew that, but that didn't stop her from running her mouth. She said what the fuck she wanted to say because she knew that she could back her shit up.

"Do you want to take his bullet for him?" I threatened.

She looked at me like I was crazy and smacked her lips. "Nigga please! You know damn well you don't scare me with all those empty threats. You ain't gonna shoot shit up in here unless you want to be in your second shootout for the night. You might not be so lucky this time though. Don't forget that you're in my hood!" She finished bandaging me up and walked out of the kitchen.

She came back with a big navy blue duffle bag. "You need to be ready for war and I got what you need," Tonya said, unzipping the bag.

The duffle bag held two AK47's, two Beretta's, and a pump. My eyes lit up when I saw the guns, extra clips, and bullets.

"Yo where the fuck you get all this shit from?"

"You know I always got what you need nigga! It's more where that came from just come back next Friday and I got you. This should be good until then. Call me if you need me Chief, you know I ain't ever been scared to bust my gun. When I shoot mine I don't miss," she winked her eye at me.

"Good looking out Tonya. How much I owe you for this shit?"

"You don't owe me nothing. Just do what you gotta do to stay alive. Let me know any information you find out about this dude so I can know who to go after in case something happens to you. Now get the fuck out of my house, I got a nigga 'bout to come over."

I gave Tonya a hug and a kiss on the cheek before I walked out of the door. I knew that if I needed her to go to war with me, she would. That bitch was loyal as hell and she was more gangster than most niggas. I knew that I had to catch Elijah before he caught me, and that was exactly what I planned on doing.

CHAPTER FIVE
Milan

It had been thirty-two days since Chief had kidnapped me and held me hostage. I knew because I had counted the sun rises and sunsets. With each day passing, my visions of Elijah coming to save me slowly started to fade. Hoping that he would find me was the only thing that kept me going. As more time went by, that glimmer of hope began to float out of the window.

I was determined not to let Chief's crazy ass win, though. I was going to get out of that hell hole one way or another. He might have won many battles, but he was not going to win the war. I was going to see to it that I got out of there, but not before I sent Chief to meet his maker.

For a month straight, Chief had raped and tortured me every night. He had tried to get me to give up Elijah's address, but I was willing to die before he got that information out of me. He would violently fuck me in the ass, burn me all over my body with blunts, and slice me with little razors. One time he even went as far as putting a lighter to my nipples which was some of the most excruciating pain in life. For about the first week, he just let me marinate in my own body fluids. I knew I was reeking because I was sitting in sweat, blood, and his nasty ass sperm, so you could only imagine how horrific the smell was. I guess he got tired of smelling me because he started giving me sponge baths every day and putting deodorant under my armpits. But he never let me get up from that chair. I was pretty damn sure that I had blisters all over my ass and the backs of my legs from sitting on that hard ass wood for a month and two days.

Unfortunately for me Chief didn't believe that I was pregnant with his baby. It was either that or he just didn't give a fuck. The sad part about it was I was due for my period two weeks prior and it still was nowhere in sight. It was ironic how every lie I had told was starting to come to pass. It was like I had spoken all the bullshit into existence. I had lied and told

Chief that I was pregnant with his baby, and there I was back in the same situation that I had just gotten out of.

Feeling sorry for myself was something that I wasn't about to do. I didn't know how long I had until Chief got back, so I had to do something quick. Then I realized that it was nothing I could do being that I was handcuffed to the damn chair.

"Fuck! I'm never going to get out of here," I cried. I heard keys jingling in the door, so I knew Chief was about to come back in. I got myself together quick because I wasn't about to let him see me sweat.

He walked through the door and he had a goofy grin on his face. I already knew what that meant. He was ready to have his way with me. Every time he touched me I wanted to throw up so I was determined not to let the shit happen again.

"All right, Chief, you win," I said in a barely audible tone.

"What did you say?" he cupped his hand around his ear as if that was going to help him hear me better.

"I said you win!" I damn near screamed it that time so I could make sure he heard me. "I'll tell you whatever you want to know about Elijah, but it's going to be on my terms."

"And why are you so confident that I'm going to agree to your terms?"

"We both want something out of this. You want information, and I want to get the fuck up out of here. So you either help me help you or we both gonna be shit out of luck."

He looked at me for a while, probably trying to figure out if he could trust me or not. I knew that he wanted Elijah dead, but it was hard to catch him slipping so he would take any piece of information he could get.

Just like I thought, Chief went for the bait. "What exactly are your terms?"

"Before I get to all of that, I need you to get me out of these handcuffs."

"Don't push it, bitch," he snapped. "I ain't agreed to shit yet, so don't get too hasty. Before I let you out of those cuffs I got some questions that I need answers to."

74

I thought about it for a minute and I figured it couldn't hurt if that's what it was going to take to get my freedom back.

"Well, what do you wanna know?"

"I wanna know why as hard as you tried to protect him after all this time, you're suddenly so willing to give him up now? You wanna know what I think? I think you're gonna try to feed me a whole bunch of bullshit just so I can let you go. You ain't as smart as you think, Milan. You might be able to get over on everybody else, but you ain't gonna get over on *me*!"

He stood over me and we both looked at each other with hate in our eyes. At that point I was ready for him to just go ahead and kill me. The only thing he was doing was prolonging my death because I knew that eventually the inevitable would occur.

CHAPTER SIX
Tiana

"Let's go, Tiana. I ain't got all day to be waiting on you!" London yelled through my door, snapping me out of the daze I was in.

I had been staring at the long scar that stretched across the side of my stomach where I had been cut open for surgery. Looking at that was a reminder of what had happened to me. I didn't look at it in a negative way, though because had I survived what could have killed someone else.

"I'm coming! I'm coming!" I shouted back to London.

I pulled the black tank top I was wearing back down over my stomach and brushed a piece of lint off my black shorts. I slid my feet in a pair of black flip flops, grabbed my wallet, and walked out of my room.

When I opened the door, London was standing right there. "It took you long enough! Girl it's hot as hell outside. You're gonna pass out with all that black on in the middle of August."

76

"I'm pretty sure the walk from the parking lot to the inside of the mall ain't gonna kill me."

I walked right past her, and she followed me down the hall. I stopped at my mom's door and peeked in to see her cuddled up with Jordan on her chest. He was the cutest baby I had ever seen because he looked just like me. I was so glad that he was finally home. With him being the only boy, he was being spoiled rotten by all of us. I could tell my mom was happier now that he was home. He had only stayed in the hospital for two weeks before he gained enough weight to leave. Besides that, he was just as healthy as a full-term baby.

"We're leaving to go to the mall, Mama. Call us if you need anything while we're out," I whispered so I wouldn't wake Jordan.

"Okay, y'all be careful," Mom said.

I grabbed the mail out of the mailbox before we left and saw a letter addressed to me. I waited until we got in London's car to open it. It was a card from my English professor and the class telling me to get well soon, and they were awaiting my return. I smacked my teeth and slapped the card down in my seat.

London looked over at me with a look of confusion on her face, "What's all that about?"

"I'm so damn sick of all this sympathy bullshit. People keep treating me like a damn victim when I don't need nobody's pity. It was fine at first, but it's been over a month. I'll be glad when people just let the shit go!"

"Well, they're just trying to be nice, Tiana. People would expect you to need and want some support. You're just always trying to be hard. I know it feels good to know that many people care about you."

"I guess you have a point. It's starting to get old. I want to just put the shit behind me, but that's hard seeing as though I get a reminder every other day."

"To me it seems like you have already put it behind you. Just think of it like this: for every well wish you receive, it's a life that you have touched in some type of way. Everyone wants you to be as amazing to you as you have been to them,"

London explained. She gave me a warm smile to go along with her kind words.

Before I knew it, we were pulling into the parking garage at Macarthur Mall in downtown Norfolk. We parked on the third floor by Nordstrom, so that was the first store we entered. As we were walking in, I noticed London looking at her phone. Whatever was in it had her smiling from ear to ear.

"What the hell are you so happy about?" I asked her.

"Didn't know I needed a reason to be happy." London shrugged and went right back in her phone.

"Well, I know my big sister. You ain't over there cheesing for nothing. Let me see what you're looking at." I snatched the phone out of London's hand before she could resist.

She tried to get it back, but I wasn't going to make it easy for her. "Stop playing, Tiana. Give me my shit back!"

"I wouldn't have had to take it if you would stop keeping secrets. I just wanna know what or *who* got my sister in such a good mood these days. You've been going on a lot of dates, staying up late talking on the phone, and your ass is even getting bigger." I pinched her on the ass, causing her to jump.

"Well what does my ass have to do with anything?" London laughed.

"You know what they say: when somebody is hitting it right, that ass gets phatter. I know somebody getting some of that London. Who you tryna fool? I'm insulted because I thought we were best friends." I pouted my lips and folded my arms like a kid about to have a temper tantrum.

"We're best friends. I just haven't told anyone because I don't know how to feel about this dude yet." London started to look through the clothing racks, trying her best to avoid me.

"Since you don't want to talk, I'll just find out for myself." I looked at London's phone in my hand, and instantly a text came through.

"Give me my phone, bitch!" London tried again to get the phone from me.

It was too late because I had already seen the text displayed on the screen. It was from someone named Elijah. He wanted London to know he had a surprise for her.

"Um…who the hell is *Elijah*, huh, London?"

"He's just a friend, Tiana. That's all."

"Where did you meet this *friend*?"

"Funny that you asked that because the first time I saw him, you were with me."

"I was? When was this?"

"It was the night that we were looking for Milan." London walked ahead of me to go to another clothing rack. By that time she already had a shit load of clothes that looked like it was weighing down her arm.

I thought back to the night that we went to look for Milan, and it was a little unclear to me at first since that was almost two months ago. Then it all came back to me.

"I know that you ain't talking about Mr. Tall, Dark, and Handsome?"

London didn't give me a direct answer, but the smirk that crept up on her face told me all that I needed to know.

I gasped. "No you didn't! I can't believe you!"

She didn't answer me, but I knew that her *friend* was dude that we had seen with Milan.

I had to pick up my pace to keep up with London's long strides. Once I caught up with her, I reached out and grabbed her arm. "Don't walk away from me, hoe!"

She snatched her arm away from me and continued walking toward the checkout line. "I'm about to buy this stuff so I can keep it moving to the next store. You're so busy hounding me that you ain't even shopping like we supposed to be doing."

I followed her to the register and stood in line beside her. She was lucky because she knew I wasn't going to cause a scene in front of all the people, but it wasn't over. I was going to get her ass to talk!

The whole time we were waiting in line London was all up in her phone. This dude was keeping her attention 24/7. All

I could do was look at her and shake my head. She was so engrossed in her phone that she didn't even notice the line moving forward.

"Pay attention and carry your ass! Lucky I ain't behind you 'cause I would have skipped you!" I said.

She waved me off and moved forward. After the cashier gave her the total, I expected her to pull out the credit card that my mom had given all of us, but instead she pulled out a wad of money. I wondered where the hell she'd gotten all that cash from, but I was almost certain it had come from her little friend.

As soon as we walked out of the store I got right back to drilling London. "You ain't getting out of this one, London. You *know* you about to hear my mouth! Talking 'bout you didn't want to tell me 'cause you don't know how you feel about him. It's pretty damn clear how you feel about him. He obviously got your ass head over heels. The real why you didn't want to tell me is because you knew damn well you were wrong and you didn't want to hear me say it! Come on.

We're going to the food court so we can sit down and talk about this."

"We can talk about it on the way home. I came here to shop not eat." London was trying to avoid the topic at all costs.

"We've only been in one store, and you've already blown a thousand dollars. I'm pretty sure these other stores can wait." with that said, I grabbed her and pulled her toward the food court. She didn't resist, so I let her arm go.

We ordered a pizza at Sbarro in the food court and went to go find a table.

"Ugh, I hate eating at the food court. These tables are always nasty," London said with her face frowned up. She spotted two of the janitors sweeping the same spot and shook her head. She walked closer to them and said, "Excuse me. Can one of y'all please come and wipe these dirty tables. There is work that needs to be done while y'all standing there trying to look busy."

I didn't know what had gotten into London. She had been acting strange, but I didn't know what was going on. After the janitor cleaned a table for us, we sat down and London wasted no time smashing the pizza.

"Talk to me, sis." I took a sip of my Coke and waited patiently for her to tell me what the fuck was going on.

"All right. I'm just going to fill you in on each and every detail. The night I confronted Milan at the bar, I went to her house later. Elijah walked up and saw me standing in front of her door and he thought I was her so I went with it," she shrugged her shoulders.

I narrowed my eyes and gave London a disapproving look, but I didn't say anything. I knew that if I interrupted her while she was in the middle of talking she would stop telling me the story.

"Anyway, the next time I talked to him, we met up and I told him the truth. I let him know that I used him to get back at Milan. Check this out, though! Milan told him a bunch of lies about how we fucked her over and that she cut us off. She even told that man that Chief was raping her? I mean can you believe that shit? That's a manipulative conniving bitch!" By then London had wolfed down two slices of pizza and was working on her third.

I shook my head in disbelief. "I don't want to believe it," I said.

London looked at me like I was crazy. "Well, you need to believe it. I don't see why you're the only one who ain't got the picture yet. Something is really wrong with Milan. I don't know what it is, but I hope she gets some help. We have never done anything to her for her to be treating us like we're the bad guys. She didn't even have the decency to come to the hospital to see about you. I know that if the shoe was on the other foot, you would've been running to her side. When Chris Brown said these hoes ain't loyal I guess that went for sisters too." London shook her head and slurped the little bit of lemonade she had left through her straw.

I couldn't even argue with London when it came to Milan. I never wanted to think that my sister would turn out the way she had. It hurt me to know that she didn't even care enough to see if I would live or die. I hadn't gotten a phone call, a visit, or nothing. She really was showing her true colors. She had been fucking up a lot of lives with her lies and deception. It was sad to say that I never really knew my sister that I lived with for almost twenty years.

"That's not the end of the story, though," London said, snapping me out of my thoughts. "What I'm about to tell you can never leave this table. You have to swear you won't open her mouth."

"Girl, you know me better than that."

"I found out from Elijah that Milan was working for Chief bringing drugs back from Maryland—"

I knew I hadn't just heard what I thought I had. "Are you fucking serious? No wonder that bitch always had all that money to splurge. I ain't gonna lie. I thought she was trickin'. I never would have thought she would do something illegal. Why the fuck would Chief even have his wife's daughter doing some shit like that anyway? See what I mean when I say

I never trusted that nigga? My instincts never steer me wrong. I still don't trust him!"

"Well, that's not what I made you promise not to tell. Chief paid somebody to murder Elijah's father and now he's trying to take Elijah out."

"What's so good about Elijah and his dad that Chief would have him killed?"

London looked around her and lowered her voice to a whisper. "You haven't put it together yet? Elijah is the *plug*! That's who Chief gets his drugs from and years back Elijah's dad was the man. You know how it goes in the game. Everybody wanna be the top dog."

I was in complete disbelief. "London what the hell do you know about the game? Not a damn thing. You got a good thing going for yourself with your degree and grad school. Don't fuck it up by getting in bed with a drug dealer. Think about it. If that's who Chief is getting his work from, imagine how many other niggas getting it from him. I wouldn't doubt that it's other motherfuckers out here who have the same mind as Chief. I don't want you getting caught up in no bullshit that don't even have anything to do with you. That ain't even you...getting involved with no drug dealers."

"Chill out. Ain't nothing going to happen to me."

"How do you know that? You're playing with fire, girl. You're messing with Milan's man who's a kingpin that also happens to have beef with your mama's soon to be ex husband. What if you happen to be with Elijah the next time him and Chief meet? Do you really think that Chief is gonna give a fuck about shooting you too?"

"Just leave it alone, Tiana. We have other things to worry about. Elijah thinks that Chief and Milan were working together to set him up because she just up and disappeared. He hasn't seen or heard from her since that night at the bar. We need to find out what's going on."

"We don't need to find out shit. I ain't got nothing to do with that. If they are working together, what does that have to do with *us*? Not a damn thing!"

"With all the shit Milan has been talking about us, there ain't no telling. You said it yourself you don't trust Chief. We both find it funny that Chief would want to help you after you shot him. Milan just up and disappeared, and he mysteriously pops back up. It's more to that story, and we need to find out what it is. If Chief has motives for popping back up, we need to know about it and be prepared."

I raised an eyebrow at London. "You went to school for the wrong thing. A detective is what you should have been."

We both laughed and started to gather our trash from the table so we could continue shopping. London had just given me an earful. But no matter how crazy my sister sounded, she always made a damn good point. Chief's return had been a problem for me. His attempt at being nice and acting like everything was cool just didn't sit right with me. I didn't know what it was, but I would never be comfortable with him around. Before I ever let anybody put another bullet in me, I wouldn't think twice about spraying them with some bullets of my own.

CHAPTER SEVEN
Silina

"Hello? May I please speak with Silina?" a raspy voice came through my phone.

"This is she. May I ask who I'm speaking with?"

"This is Patrice. You remember Shawn's big sister?"

My skin crawled when I heard his name. I was glad that the bastard was dead. I hadn't heard from his sister in almost fifteen years, and I couldn't help but wonder what she wanted.

"Of course I remember you. How could I forget? To what do I owe the pleasure of this call?"

"I'm sure you've heard by now that my brother was killed. I don't know all the details because I just found out that he had been cremated a couple of weeks back. I know that you and the girls are distraught, but I just wanted to let you know that I'm here for you if you need me."

I rolled my eyes and held back from saying what I really wanted to say. Instead I just said, "We will get through it."

"I called to tell you that Shawn had a life insurance policy that he made sure I kept up with. You're the beneficiary of the policy, so nobody can touch it without you."

I was taken aback by what Patrice had just told me. Shawn had spent his whole bid in jail thinking that I was the one who had set him up, but he still made it his business to leave something to me and our girls in case anything ever happened to him.

"Well, what do I need to do?" I asked.

"You need to contact the insurance company and send in a copy of the death certificate. I have a copy of it that I can fax over to you. Then they will ask you to submit a claim once everything goes through you will have access to the money."

"Okay send me all the information I'll need and I will keep you posted."

"I'll fax everything over to you just text me your fax number and you'll have everything within the hour. Tell my nieces I love them and that I will be seeing them very soon."

"All right. I'll talk to you later, Trice!"

Patrice had always been a greedy little bitch, and I knew that the only reason she had told me about the policy was because she wanted a piece of the pie. I knew it wasn't because she loved and cared about her nieces because as soon as Shawn, aka her ATM machine, got locked up, she disappeared. I already knew what Patrice had up her sleeve, but I wasn't worried because it wasn't like we desperately needed the money anyway.

I heard the doorbell ring and I looked at my baby boy who was still peacefully sleeping in his bassinet. I got out of my bed, turned the baby monitor on, and went downstairs to see who was ringing my doorbell unannounced.

I looked through the peephole and saw Chief standing on my porch. The scar on his face was hideous as ever, and I was annoyed by the fact that he popped up whenever he damn well pleased.

I swung the door open and stood there with my hand on my hip. "What do you want, Chief?"

"I want my son. What the fuck do you think I want?"

"Well, *my* baby is asleep. You need to stop popping up over here whenever you feel like it. You don't live here no more, so you need to call before you just make an appearance."

He moved me to the side and stepped into the house like I had given him a personal invitation. "As long as my son is living here, I'm gonna come whenever I want to. It ain't like you let me take him with me. Besides, this is still my damn house. I paid for the motherfucker!'

"Can you prove that you paid for it? Do you have a legitimate source of income that can verify that you make enough to afford this house? I didn't think so, please stop trying me, Chief. You don't know nothing about taking care of a premature infant. I'd be a fool to let my son leave this house with you!"

"You can either make this easy or we can settle this shit in court. I'm not gonna just sit back and allow you to keep my son away from me!"

"I'm not keeping him from you. I just said you ain't taking him with you and I meant that. Don't even stand here and act like I don't let you see him because frankly, I get sick of seeing your face. You can try the court shit if you want to, but we both know that you won't win. I know damn well you ain't trying to go up in no courts and have them people all in your business. If they dig too deep, they might find a little more than they bargained for," I warned him.

I would never try to keep Jordan away from Chief because I knew that my son needed his father. I was just overprotective of my baby. He was only six weeks old and he was born nine weeks early, so I had every reason to be. I didn't mind him coming over to spend time with him, but a phone call would be nice.

Chief scowled at me and started walking toward the stairs.

I was right on his heels as he started walking up the stairs. "I just told you he was asleep. He's been up all day fussing, and you are not about to go in there and wake him up."

"I just want to see him. Damn girl! I won't wake him up."

"If you just wanted to see him I could have sent you a damn picture," I replied sarcastically.

He walked over to Jordan's bassinet and stood over him. A heart-warming smile spread across his face as he watched his son sleep. I couldn't deny the love he had for his son, and it was a beautiful thing, but I just couldn't get with Chief. No matter how hard he tried, I would never give him another chance. I couldn't get the image of him and Milan out of my head.

I walked out of the room when I realized that Chief wasn't going to wake him up. I let him get his quality time in because that popping up shit was going to come to an end. I went in the kitchen and grabbed a Seagrams Jamaican Me Happy out of the refrigerator before I sat down on the couch. I remembered that I was supposed to be texting Trice my fax number so I sent it over to her while I was thinking about it. I flipped through the channels and an argument between Cynthia and NeNe from Real Housewives of Atlanta caught my attention.

I got so caught up in the show and sipping my little wine cooler that I didn't even pay Chief any mind when he came in the living room. That was until I felt a hand creeping up my thigh.

I slapped his hand like I was killing a bug. "Nigga, are you *crazy*? You got to be sniffing that shit you out there selling."

"Stop trying to fight it, Silina. You know you still love me, girl. The type of love we have doesn't just die. No matter what we will always be a part of each other. You'll always be my number one lady."

I couldn't help but to laugh in his face because he couldn't be serious. "Nice try, wrong woman, honey. Stop trying to come on to me, Chief because the only cock I want from you is your John Hancock, on these damn divorce papers!"

"Was that supposed to be a joke because I didn't find it funny it all."

"It wasn't meant to be funny, but it was real. You will never get a chance to taste this again, so you better keep up with the memories of the shit I could do to you." I smirked. "I'm ready to move on with my life, but you're holding me up.

"What do you mean move on with your life? You got another nigga or something? You know I'm not gonna deal with another nigga around my son!"

"What I do is no longer any of your concern. You have nothing to worry about, though because I will never bring another man around my kids. The last time I did that he ended up fucking one of them."

"I know I fucked up, Silina, but I have been good to you for years. I have *never* done you wrong, and I did everything in my power to show you how much I cherished you. You're the most beautiful woman I have ever met inside and out. You know you were a nigga's backbone, and I miss that. I know out of all those years, I get room for one fuck up. I know you can do some soul searching and find it in your heart to forgive me."

I leaned in closer to him and whispered seductively in his ear, "You know what you're right. I could…but I'm not."

His reaction made me want to fall over laughing because I knew he thought he was about to get some ass. Since he wanted to keep fucking with me I decided to have a little fun with him.

He got up and adjusted his hard dick in his pants. "You know what? I'm out. I'll be back through here to check on my lil man."

"Make sure you call next time. Bye!"

I followed him to the door, and as he was leaving out, London was coming in. She rushed past me like she was in a marathon with her hand covering her mouth. I locked the door and ran to the bathroom behind her. When I walked in, she was emptying the contents of her stomach in the toilet.

I grabbed a wash cloth, ran cold water on it, and started wiping her face with it.

"Are you ok baby?" I asked.

"I feel much better now. I think it was something I ate." She gently started shoving me out of the bathroom. "Now if you'll excuse me I need to brush my teeth."

I walked out of the bathroom, but I didn't leave. I stood outside the door and listened. I heard her cut the water on and fiddle around in the medicine cabinet. A couple of seconds later I heard her throwing up again. I went back in the bathroom and she was standing over the sink throwing up this time.

I put my hand on her forehead and checked to see if she had a fever. I rubbed her back while she regurgitated. A mother's job was never done even if her kids were grown. I wanted to be sure that my daughter was fine.

When she finished throwing up everywhere I took her upstairs to her room and made her lay down. I went back to the kitchen and grabbed her some saltine crackers and ginger ale. I had to make her eat a couple of the crackers and drink the soda.

"If you're not feeling any better by the morning, I'm taking you to the hospital." I said.

"I don't need to go to the hospital, Ma. Now get out of here because if I do have something contagious I don't want my baby brother to get it."

She was right, so I left her room and went to take a shower and relax before Jordan woke up for another bottle. After I got comfortable, I went in my office to see if Patrice had faxed over the death certificate. Sure enough, the fax had come through.

When I looked at what she'd sent, I realized that not only had she sent over his death certificate and the claim form for the insurance company, but also some medical records from St. Brides, the prison he was locked up in. Curiosity got the best of me, and I looked through the medical records.

From what I read, Shawn was being treated by a psychiatrist while he was locked up. I read something that said 'The patient displays signs of a psychopath.' I read further to see that the diagnosis was positive.

"Oh shit! I had lived with and birthed children with a psychopath!"

I instantly turned on my computer and started doing some research. I'll be damned if Shawn didn't show practically every sign of a psychopath. I didn't know why I had been so blind to it. I had heard about the condition and seen things on TV, but I had never thought that I would actually meet someone who had it. I really started to get worried when I saw that it was genetic. I hoped to God that none of my girls had picked up the trait from him.

CHAPTER EIGHT
Chief

I was leaving from Silina's crib with a lot of heavy shit on my mind. I knew I had fucked up by putting my dick up in Milan, but I never thought we would get caught. I should have known better than to fuck her daughter in the house in our bed, but what can I say? I was thinking with my dick instead of my brain, and that had caused me to lose the woman that I loved and mother of my child.

Even though I knew I was wrong, I still thought that she would eventually forgive me because no matter what I did to any of those other bitches I used to deal with, they always came running back. Silina was different, but I wasn't going to let go that easily. Every man had a weakness and Silina, and now my lil man Jordan, was mine.

It was easy for me to take all my built up frustrations out on Milan because I felt like it was her fault that I had lost my family. Milan never knew when to stop running her mouth and she had told it all. She would have never been in the situation she was in now if she wouldn't have tried to be a gangsta bitch and pull out a gun on me. Better believe that any nigga that ever pulled out a pistol on me got sent to their maker, and I damn sure wasn't about to have no bitch thinking she could get away with it.

I'll admit that when I saw her with Elijah I didn't know what the fuck was going on. For a second I was like, *Damn! She didn't waste no time hopping on my connect's dick.* Shit had me fucked up at first then I told myself she wasn't my lady. I didn't plan on hurting her when I saw her with Elijah, my main target was him.

Elijah had been my plug since I had his father, Big John, murked years ago. Shit didn't go as I had planned it because I was hoping that with his pops out of the picture, I could take over the east coast. Big John had everywhere from New York down to Florida on lock. I ran the 757 and had clout in D.C., but that wasn't enough for me. I wanted it all.

I thought that when Big John was out the way, I could start moving in on his territory. The only thing that stopped me was the fact that with Big John being gone, Elijah's bitch ass stepped up. The problem with Elijah was he had one thing that I didn't: a Columbian connect.

It didn't take me no time to get them bricks gone, and before I knew it I had to re-up again. Niggas were never trying to give up their plug, so I had to start copping from Elijah. I watched him rise to the top. After a short time, he was making it snow from the east to the west. Within a year, he had far exceeded what Big John had done in the game. Elijah was smarter because he never dealt directly with anyone but me, so no one had ever seen his face.

A nigga like me wasn't down for working up under no young cat. He was fucking up the game by selling his bricks for dirt cheap, and it was always some fish scale. That made it hard for all of the other hustlers that were trying to come up in the game because people would rather pay his price for the best quality shit. My plan was to get closer to Elijah so that he could trust me. I knew that he was going to eventually want to step out of the game and go legit. I was hoping that since I was his right hand man, he would put me in with the Columbian connects, but after a few years it didn't look like that was going to happen. I knew I had to switch up my plan, and that's when I decided to just take everything he had and kill him.

I drove back to the cabin I owned deep in Suffolk where I was holding Milan hostage. When I walked in she was sitting in the chair I had her tied up to looking pitiful. I almost felt sorry for her, and then I remembered that if it hadn't been for a gun being put to her head, she would have killed me.

"I know you want to get out of here, Milan. I can let you go, but only if you're willing to help me."

"What the fuck do you want from me, Chief?" she asked.

"You're going to help me get Tiana."

Her eyes widened at the mention of her sister's name. "Ain't no way in hell I will help you do something like that! Tiana is still my sister, and I won't have any part in setting her up, so you might as well just kill me. I'm ready to die anyway, so fuck it! And fuck you too!" Leave my sister the fuck alone, you psychotic bitch!" she spit at my feet.

"Okay, Milan. Don't ever say I didn't try to help you. I tried to give you a chance to go free, but it doesn't matter to me whether you take it or not. I can get Tiana with or without you. That lil bitch shot me, and she ain't getting away with it! So I guess both of y'all just have to suffer."

I meant what I had said too. Tiana was going to pay for what she had done. I didn't plan on killing her because I knew that Silina's poor little heart couldn't take any more pain. There would be some type of consequence for her actions, though. It took me months to get back right after she shot me in the chest. If it hadn't been for my homey, Black, sending somebody to help me, I would have died in that room. The only reason why I had saved Tiana from her dad killing her was because I wanted to kill her myself.

"You need to just let it go, Chief. She was trying to protect her mom. Wouldn't you have done the same if you could?"

When I heard her mention my mama I punched her in her jaw so hard blood flew from her mouth. I didn't like for motherfuckers to speak on my moms because she was no longer here, and I missed her like crazy. It was because of me that her and my pops were killed. Some fuck nigga tried to get at me, but when they couldn't get to me, he went to my mom and pop's house and murdered them. The streets are always talking, so it didn't take me long to find the bitch ass nigga who did it. When I did find out it was a bloody massacre in the streets of Norfolk. I killed him and everybody connected with that motherfucker, but that didn't bring my parents back.

Milan was crying and rubbing the side of her cheek. That shit didn't move me at all. Maybe her ass would learn to watch her fucking mouth. I was getting bored playing games with her. I didn't know why I hadn't killed her ass, but since she wasn't trying to help me, her life was now on a countdown.

My phone rang, and I left Milan sitting in the living room by herself to take the call. I saw that it was my right hand man, Black, and I knew he had some information for me.

"Talk to me," I answered.

"Ya boy, Elijah, is on his way to pick up them bricks, and I'm following him now. This is our chance to get this nigga."

"Where you at now?"

"We're up in Maryland. I followed the nigga from VA here. I overheard one of my niggas saying that they were waiting for their plug to get back to Maryland with them bricks, and I know they were talking about Elijah."

"You know what to do." I hung up the phone.

If it wasn't for the fact that they were almost three hours away, I would have been the one to take everything from Elijah and let him look his killer in the eye before I pulled the trigger. For now, my nigga would have to be the one to get the job done.

Elijah

One thing I realized that niggas didn't know about me was that I was always five steps ahead of them. It had been a while since I put my murder game down, so I guess niggas thought that I didn't have it in me anymore. That's where they had shit fucked up at. When I was leaving from spending time with London in VA to go handle some business, I noticed that someone was following me. They didn't even try to fall back and follow me from a distance. They were right on my ass. Every time I switched lanes, so did they. When I sped up, they sped up too.

"This nigga gotta be the dumbest motherfucker I've ever seen!"

What he didn't know was that he was about to follow me right into a trap. My instincts were telling me that this had something to do with Chief. I couldn't see who was in the car because it was all black with dark tints and it was dark outside. They made sure they stayed behind me and never rode beside me. I grabbed my phone and called my nigga, Ox. He was the only nigga I trusted because I knew that his loyalty to me ran deep. He was the one niggas dealt with when they wanted to get drugs from me.

"What's good, boss? That shipment is about to come in. Are you on your way?"

"Yeah, fam. I'm like thirty minutes from you now. It looks like we're expecting company too. Some nigga followed me all the way from VA. I know they think they're about to take what I got and try to kill me, so this is what I want you to do. When the delivery truck comes in, I want you to handle that for me. I'm going to drive this nigga around town to buy some time before I bring him back to you. Hit me up when you unload everything."

"I got you, boss."

After driving around for another hour or so, Ox finally called me back and told me he was done. I always had the bricks delivered to my soul food restaurant, Pop's Kitchen, in a food truck. That way it looked like we were just getting our weekly inventory for the restaurant.

I pulled up in the back of my restaurant and turned my car off. I reached under my seat and grabbed the glock I kept under there. I checked my surroundings, and I didn't notice anything that looked funny. My restaurant was closed, so there weren't any people around. And it was pitch black in the back alley where I was parked. I didn't see the car that had been following me anymore, but I knew that something was up with that. The person probably parked somewhere else trying to be inconspicuous, not knowing that I was already on to him.

I got out of my car to go through the back door that led to The Dungeon, which was the basement inside my restaurant. I'd had sound proof walls installed just in case some shit needed to go down. You couldn't get through the steel door that led to the Dungeon from the inside of my restaurant unless you had a code, so I wasn't worried about anyone ever finding out about the room.

Just when I approached the back door a man dressed in all black tried to run up on me. He was a small motherfucker, probably about 5'8". So I stood over him by at least 7 inches.

He had on a ski mask, but I could still see his eyes, and that was all I needed to see. The more I looked at him, the more I realized who he was.

This is the same nigga that was with Chief the first time that he was shooting at me. I knew I was right about this shit.

"You know what the fuck this is, nigga. Get your ass in the door and give it up, bitch!" the man said, waving his pistol around.

I couldn't do anything but laugh at the lil nigga. When I looked in his eyes I didn't see nothing but a bitch ass nigga.

"What the fuck is so funny, motherfucker? This shit ain't no game. Don't make me put a bullet in yo ass!" he pointed his gun in my face.

"I don't think you're gonna do that for real for two reasons. Number one you just told me to "give it up" so I know that you want what I got and if you shoot me you'll never find out where it is. Number two is because I think you're a bitch."

Before he even knew what had happened, I sucker punched him so hard that I knocked him out, and the gun fell out of his hand. Ox was coming out the door, and saw him still lying on the ground. I knew that he wasn't going to try to get up because he was really scared without his gun. He was probably realizing that he had gotten himself in a fucked up situation.

They didn't call my nigga Ox for no reason. He was big, black, and strong as a fuckin' ox. He leaned down and punched the nigga on the ground one more time before we picked him up and carried him into the Dungeon.

Ox threw him in a chair, and when he tried to tie his arms up, he started trying to put up a little bit of a fight. That didn't do shit but make things worse for him. Ox used him as a punching bag, sending blows all over his face, head, and body.

"Can you give us a minute, Ox?" I asked and he excused himself from the room.

I went and stood in front of the nigga who had tried to rob me. "Who the fuck sent you here, bitch?" I asked already knowing the answer, but I wanted to see if he would tell the truth.

"Fuck you, bitch! I ain't telling yo bitch ass shit!" he spit a glob of blood at my feet.

"That's the wrong answer, motherfucker." I walked over to the closet where I kept an arsenal of weapons and grabbed a machete. I stood in his face again and bent down so that I could look him right in his eyes. "Now tell me what the fuck I want to know or yo ass is going to lose a limb until there's nothing left of your ass. Who the hell are you and who sent you?"

He frowned his face up but still didn't say a word. Since the motherfucker thought I was playing I took the machete and sliced one of his fingers off. Blood splattered all over my fresh wife beater.

"Aaargh what the fuck, man?" he screamed out in pain, sounding like the bitch he was.

"Still don't have anything to say?" I asked.

"Fuck you! You might as well kill me because I ain't telling you shit!"

I nodded my head and said, "Okay," before I sliced his whole right hand off with the machete. The blood started pouring out like a fountain.

This time the nigga started crying like a lil ass girl. I don't know what the fuck made him think that it would be that easy to just get at a nigga like me. Chief must have gassed him up. Either that or he was trying to gain some cool points with him, but the only thing that was going to happen was him getting sent back to Chief in a body bag.

"This is the last time I'm gonna ask you. Who sent you?"

He still didn't answer me so I sliced him across his neck with the machete, damn near decapitating him. He died with his eyes still open, looking right at me. I wiped the blood off of my machete and put it back in my weapon's closet. I went in his pockets and took his cell phone at. When I looked in his call log I saw that he had called Chief a few times within the past couple of hours. I went to his name and pressed the send button on the cell phone.

"What's good, Black? Did you get his ass?"

I didn't feel anything but rage when I heard his voice. "No, but I'm coming to get you," I warned him and hung up the phone. Chief didn't know that he had started a war.

CHAPTER NINE
London

"Are you ready to leave yet, beautiful?" Elijah asked me while I was standing in the mirror checking myself out.

"Yeah, I'm ready. Let me grab my purse."

We had taken a spur of the moment trip to Atlanta and we were staying at the Westin downtown. Our room had a lovely view of the city, and I was ready to explore. I checked myself out one last time to make sure a hair wasn't out of place or my red lipstick hadn't smeared. I must say that I looked gorgeous in my red romper pantsuit with some nude colored red bottoms. My natural hair was styled into a bob with feathered bangs. Thanks to Elijah, I had diamonds draped around my neck and dangling from my earlobes. Once I was satisfied with my look, I grabbed my clutch that matched perfectly with my shoes, and we were out the door.

Elijah kept it simple, yet he still matched my fly. He was rocking a pair of black jeans with some black and red

Jordan's. He had on a red Ralph Lauren Polo shirt and he was iced out with his watch, pinky ring, and earrings.

We took the exterior elevator up to the 72nd floor where the Sun Dial restaurant was located. The scenery on the way up was nothing short of breath taking. It was night time, so the city was lit up and it made a beautiful sight. Elijah and I were talking and laughing the whole way up. We started growing closer after I told him the truth about who I was. Initially, I believed that he only wanted to use me to get information about Chief, but after a while he didn't even ask me about that fool anymore. We were nothing more than friends, but he treated me like I was his woman, and I was fine with that. I was starting to think that he was really feeling me, and I was definitely feeling him.

We finally entered the restaurant and I was impressed. There was a panoramic view, and the restaurant did a 360 degree rotation, so while you were eating you could see the entire city. We decided to sit right by one of the floor to ceiling windows. Elijah pulled out my chair and pushed me in before he went to go sit down.

When Elijah sat across from me he stared intensely into my eyes. "It's something that I need to talk to you about."

The way he looked at me had me about ready to melt. I could feel the sexual tension between us, and I was ready to give in to temptation. I don't know if it was the romantic ambiance of the place, the sex appeal that Elijah had, or the fact that I hadn't had sex in three months, when I had tricked Elijah into fucking me. All I knew was I was ready to put this pretty thang on him.

"What is it?'

As soon as he opened his mouth to talk a waiter approached our table. We told him that we needed a minute and that we would let him know when we were ready to order. Elijah did order a bottle of wine, though, and the waiter brought it right out.

Before he started talking again, he poured us both a glass of wine. He drunk his in one swallow, but I didn't touch mine.

"You and I both know that there is an undeniable chemistry between us. I know that I was just dealing with your sister, and after what happened with her, I thought I would never trust a bitch again. The more time I spent around you, I started feeling you more than I was supposed to. The same gut feeling that was telling me that Milan wasn't right is the same feeling that's telling me I would be a fool to not take a chance with you. We've been getting to know each other as friends for the past three months, and I'm ready to take it up a notch if that's okay with you."

I was completely floored by what he'd said. I had no idea that when he announced that he wanted to talk, he would be asking me to be his lady. For a moment I was at a loss for words. "I don't know what to say, Elijah. To be honest, I've been feeling you since the first time I was in your presence. The vibe I got was indescribable, and it was nothing that I ever felt before. For some reason, even though I didn't know you at all, I felt like I had known you all my life. What about Milan, though? What if she just pops back up and tries to pick up where y'all left off. Where would that leave me? I can't deal with another broken heart."

"Milan is dead to me. You don't have to worry about her. You're the one I should have met first. You and I crossed each other's paths for a reason."

By that time I was smiling from ear to ear. "I have some news I have to share with you also. It's something that I haven't told anyone else."

"Oh yeah? What's that?"

"I'm three months pregnant. That night back at Milan's place…"

It didn't seem to register to him at first. Then he got real excited. "Oh shit! You mean to tell me you're having *my* baby?"

"That's exactly what I'm telling you."

He got up from his chair and came and grabbed me out of mine. He said fuck the food and escorted me back to our hotel room. As soon as we got the door closed, he put his soft lips against mine. At first he just gave me a series of pecks, and then I felt his tongue part my lips. Our tongues did a tango, and I got weak in the knees. The only thing that kept me from hitting the floor was the fact that his strong arms were wrapped around my waist.

Our kiss seemed to last for an eternity as our hands explored each others bodies. The tips of his fingers sent tingles down my spine. He broke away from my lips and started nibbling on my earlobe. Feeling him breathing in my ear got my juices flowing. Next he started licking and sucking on my neck, causing moans to escape my lips. He slid my romper off with ease then literally swept me off my feet and carried me to the couch.

He sat me on the couch and he got on the floor, directly between my legs. His soft, juicy lips latched on to my nipples, and his tongue left wet circles around them. While he was licking and sucking he put two fingers inside of me. I could feel my nectar sliding down the crack of my ass and onto the couch.

My heart was about to beat out of my chest from anticipation. Elijah's lips and tongue traveled down south until they got to the destination they were trying to reach. His lips were like a vacuum attached to my clit. The feeling was so intense that it caused me to try to push away from him. He pulled me closer to him and started licking relentlessly. I was taken by surprise when he took a piece of ice from the ice bucket and put it in his mouth. He then went right back to eating my pussy like it was a meal, with the ice in his mouth.

"Oooh yes, Elijah! I love this shit!" The pleasure he was giving me made me cum over and over and over to the point where I lost count.

When he finally came up for air, his face was saturated in my sticky wetness. He used his shirt to wipe it off and then snatched his shirt off. He took off his shoes and came out of his pants and boxers. His manhood was sticking straight out and he came and opened my legs as wide as they could go. When he slid inside me, we both took in the feeling of pure ecstasy.

"Damn, this some good pussy, ma," he groaned.

He started off with slow strokes and my pussy was gripping on that dick like pliers. The more he sped up, the more I fucked him right back. He was throwing that dick up in me and I was throwing it right back at him.

"Oooh yes! Please don't stop! Keep it right there!" he was hitting the spot that caused my whole body to quiver. "Harder, Elijah, harder! Aaaahhh I'm about to cum!"

He sped up his strokes and I came all over his dick, but he still wasn't finished. My body had never stopped shaking from the last orgasm, and after that they were coming back to back. He flipped me over and made me lay on my stomach. He entered me from behind and started fucking the shit out of me. He grabbed my hair and pulled my head back so he could whisper in my ear.

"That's right, girl. Take all this dick."

After a few more strokes I felt him pull his dick out and nut all over my ass cheeks. I couldn't do anything but lie in the same spot and try to get myself together. He got up and went to the bathroom and returned with a soapy rag to clean me off. He gently wiped my butt cheeks and between my legs.

He got back on the couch with me and pulled me on top of him. I lay on his chest and we stayed silent for a moment. The only sound I heard was the beating of his heart, which just so happened to be in sync with mine.

"You don't even know that you just made all my dreams come true. I have a beautiful woman by my side who is about to be the mother of my child. I can't believe it. I'm gonna be a daddy."

I looked up at him. He was smiling from ear to ear. When I was in his arms I felt complete. Before I knew it, we both fell asleep in each others arms.

The next morning Elijah woke me up to breakfast in bed. There was a tray of eggs, bacon, sausage, potatoes, French toast, fruit salad, and a glass of orange juice in front of me.

"I know all this food ain't for me," I said.

"You're right. It ain't just for you. It's for you and my baby. I'm going to make sure my ladies eat good," he said, grinning.

"Your *ladies*? What makes you so sure that we're going to have a girl?"

"I'm not sure, but I would love to have a little princess to spoil. Daddy's little girl." He put his hands on my stomach.

"I want a girl too so I can dress her up like me and put pretty bows and ribbons in her hair. As long as we have a healthy baby, I'll be happy."

"I'm already happy. Now eat that food so we can leave. We have shit to do today."

All that food on the plate didn't stand a chance. I ate everything down to the last morsel. Then I hopped in the shower and got dressed. We headed to Lenox Square Mall, and I tore that motherfucker up. Elijah bought me so much shit from jewelry to designer handbags to a boat load of clothes. He couldn't understand why a pregnant lady needed so many pairs of heels, but I was a shoe addict. I had so many shopping bags that we had to make trips back to the car to put them in the trunk before we could finish shopping. I was determined not to leave until I went into very single store.

After about five hours of shopping, we sat down in the food court and ate at Chick-Fil-A.

"I'm really enjoying myself here with you." I admitted.

"I bet your ass is after putting a hurting on my bank account." He laughed.

I laughed with him. "Never bring a lady to the mall and tell her to get whatever she wants because you better believe she's going to do just that."

A group of teenage girls walked past us, and I caught them giving Elijah the eye. One of the little girls was even bold enough to say, "Damn! He is fine."

"You got the young girls about to break their necks to get a glimpse of that sexual chocolate. They're lusting for you in the worst way." I giggled.

We finished up our lunch and went back to the hotel so I could get some rest. My feet and ankles were killing me from walking around that mall all day. When I laid down in the bed Elijah took off my shoes and socks and started massaging my feet and calf muscles. It was so soothing to me that I drifted off into a peaceful slumber.

I woke up about two hours later and overheard Elijah engaged in a phone conversation. I couldn't make out what he was saying, but the tone of his voice let me know that he was pissed. The look on his face confirmed that.

"Is everything okay, Elijah?"

"My nigga just told me he saw Chief and Milan together. They were outside of my house in Maryland. Get up and pack your shit. You're about to go home. I'm getting ready to give these two motherfuckers the surprise of their lives."

CHAPTER TEN
Milan

The moment that I saw London and Elijah walking hand in hand smiling like a happy couple was the moment that my heart turned cold for good. At first I didn't want to believe it because I knew that Chief would tell me anything to get me to give Elijah up. When he showed me a picture of the two of them together, I stopped breathing for what seemed like an eternity.

"What the fuck is this? What the hell is London doing with my man?" I couldn't control the tears that escaped my eyes.

I guess karma really was a bitch because I was feeling exactly what my mama was feeling when she caught me and Chief in her bed. I probably felt worse because there wasn't shit that I could do about it.

"Ain't it funny how the nigga that you were loyal to is the same nigga that just cut you—in your heart that is." Chief laughed, using the same words I said to him against me.

"Fuck you, Chief! I don't find shit funny!"

"That's too bad because I do. If you would have taken me to the nigga when I asked you to, you wouldn't have to worry about him fucking your sister because he would be dead."

"I'll do it."

"You'll do what?"

"I'll take you to him, but only under one condition."

"Here you go with your conditions and all this other bullshit. Understand that I don't need your help, but you do need mine."

"If you don't need my help then, why is Elijah still alive if you want him dead so bad? And why are you keeping me alive? It seems to me like you do need my help more than you would like to admit."

I shut Chief's ass up because no matter how much he denied it, he knew that I was right.

"What the fuck is your condition?"

"I want to pull the trigger on Elijah and London. They fucked me over in the worst way, and now it's time to pay the piper."

Chief looked at me and shook his head, laughing like I was a joke. "Well isn't that the pot calling the kettle black. I'll tell you what, do whatever you want with London. I'm gonna be the one to send Elijah to meet his maker. This is personal for me. I'll let you watch, though." A devilish grin formed on his face.

I agreed to take Chief right to the place that Elijah laid his head. I couldn't believe he had the audacity to get with my sister. It was like he just gave up on me and replaced me with her. I started to wonder if he ever came looking for me or if he was ever even worried. It was no telling what London had told him about me, but I was pretty sure all of the lies I'd told him had come out. My heart was filled with so much rage, and I was hell bent on revenge. I was determined to show Elijah and London exactly who the baddest twin was.

When Chief finally untied my legs from the chair and I tried to stand up I fell right back down. If I didn't know any better I would have thought that my legs had been replaced with oodles of noodles. My entire backside was numb, and it felt like my ass had flattened like a pancake. The skin around my ankles had turned a nasty bluish purple color from the rope being so tight. Some of my skin had even rubbed off, and for the first time I noticed how much weight I had lost. I looked sick, and I was disgusted with myself. Chief help me get into his Escalade truck, but he never took the handcuffs off me.

Having to sit right back down had me feeling like a child who had just gotten their ass whipped with a belt and having to sit on it. I wanted so badly to be put out of my misery, but I had business to tend to. I was on a murder mission and I had three people on my list whose names where Elijah, London, and Chief.

I was willing to help him get to Elijah, but what he didn't know was when he got there, he wouldn't be coming back either. I didn't have a plan, but I knew that before it was all said and done, Chief's ass was dead.

After three hours of riding in the car, we finally made it to Elijah's condo in Bethesda.

"You're going to have to take these cuffs off me, Chief. I can't do shit with these on!"

"I'll take them off, but I swear if you try anything, I'll shoot you right in the back," he warned, and I knew that he wasn't lying.

"I won't try anything, Chief. I'm here to help you," I assured him, trying to get him to trust me a little. I figured it was better for him to believe that I was on his side for the moment.

He took the cuffs off of me. They had done more damage to my wrists than the rope had to my ankles. A lot of the skin was coming off and there was dried up blood and cuts all over from me struggling to get out of them. I tried to move them around to get the blood back flowing, but it hurt like hell. I was more than ready to get this over with so that Chief could experience the same torture he had put me through for the past three months.

"So what do we do next?" I wondered out loud.

"We wait until we see the motherfucker. We'll wait right here until we catch him coming in or out. From our position, there's no way he can get past us without us seeing him. We can't just run up in the nigga's crib because I know they have cameras up in that bitch."

I didn't feel one bit of remorse for what I was about to do. For my entire life, nobody had ever given a fuck about my feelings. So now it was time for me to show motherfuckers who I really was. I was going to get my respect one way or another.

We sat in the same spot for hours and had no luck. Elijah never showed up at his condo so I figured we would go to the next best place: his restaurant. By the time we got to the restaurant, it was closed, and there wasn't a car in sight. It was pitch black inside so I knew that no one was in there.

"Fuck! You brought me on this dummy mission, and I bet as soon as we left the nigga came home!"

"Well, do you have a better idea?"

"No, I don't. I got shit I need to handle back in VA, so we gonna take this trip again in a few days. I won't need you the next time because I know where he works and where he sleeps. You'll just be in the way."

"Well, are you going to take me home when we get back to VA? I have some business to handle myself. I told you what you wanted to know, and we had a deal."

"Yeah, yeah, I'll let you go home," he said.

We rode back to VA in silence. Once we reached Northern Virginia, we stopped at a gas station. The gas station reminded me of one in a scary movie where there were no other people around for miles, and it gave me the creeps. We were completely surrounded by woods, and in the pitch black night they looked like they never ended. The only person there was a white man who was standing behind the counter chewing tobacco.

My gut was telling me that I couldn't trust Chief to take me home like he had said he would. So when he went to pay for the gas, I climbed out of the truck and made a run for it. I didn't know where the fuck I was or where I was going. I was just hoping that I would run into someone that would help me. It felt like I was moving in slow motion trying to get away from that truck and out of Chief's sight. I couldn't run as fast as I would have liked because my ankles were on fire.

Something told me not to look back, but I did anyway. Chief was running after me. I tried to speed up, but I ended up tripping over a tree branch and falling flat on my face. He caught up to me in three seconds flat and grabbed my ankles, pulling me back to him. My knees and arms were getting scraped up from all the rocks, twigs, and whatever else was on the ground. I kicked and tried my hardest to fight, but it was to no avail. He overpowered me and I was helpless once again.

"You had to try to run didn't you, bitch!"

Before I realized what was happening, he picked up a brick and started hitting me on the head with it. I saw images of me from a child all the way up to that very moment. I saw my mom and my sisters staring at me with disapproving looks on their faces. I didn't see the white light that people often said they saw when they were crossing over to the other side. All I saw was blackness and I knew that I was on my way to hell. I felt the blood pouring from my head and I felt my life slipping away from me. I didn't even try to fight it. I welcomed death with open arms.

Chief

I hauled ass back to my truck, jumped in that bitch, and took off. I left Milan's body right where it was. I burned rubber, trying to make it back to the 757 before somebody saw me.

I had gotten the information I needed from Milan. I had planned to kill her anyway because I didn't need her anymore. I had an advantage over Elijah because I knew everything about him, but he knew nothing about me. As much as it hurt me not to see my son, I even fell back from going to Silina's because I knew that he and London were dealing with each other. I couldn't put my son or wife in harm's way.

Making sure that I killed Elijah was more than business now, it was *personal*. He had slit my nigga, Black's, throat and sent his body back to his mom's house. I was going to make sure I avenged his death. I would never forgive myself because deep down inside I knew that my nigga had died for me. Elijah didn't want him, he wanted me, but Black didn't give me up. That shit had my head fucked up.

I went home, took a shower, and changed my clothes before I ended up at a bar. Ironically, Tiana was at the same bar with London's hood rat friend, Ty. They were sitting at a table talking and giggling, and I could tell they were already tipsy. Everybody I had something against was falling right into my lap. I was going to take advantage of this perfect opportunity to pay Tiana's ass back.

Before I could be noticed, I went back to my car and got a bottle of Percocet pills that I kept in the glove box. I took five of them out and crushed them up until they turned into powder. Then I made my way back inside the bar. I ordered two drinks from the bartender and poured the drugs into one of the cups. I stirred it up until it dissolved in the drink and then I walked over to the table they were sitting at.

As soon as I got close to them and Tiana noticed me, she turned her nose up at me. "What the fuck are you doing here?" she asked.

"Well, this is a public bar ain't it?" I laughed. "I came over to make peace with you, Tiana. I forgive you for what you did, so it's no need to still be holding a grudge against me." I handed them the drinks, making sure Tiana took the one with the drugs. "Have a drink on me, and let's kill all the bad blood between us. What do you say? For the sake of Jordan."

For a minute she looked like she was trying to figure out if she could trust me or not, then she said, "I don't know if I can trust you, Chief, but I'll think about it over this drink."

I watched her down the laced drink and walked away from the table. I sat at the bar and waited for the Percocet to kick in. I knew that it would knock her out cold. It didn't take long for the drugs to take effect. I saw her nodding off. It appeared that Ty was asking if she was okay. I walked over to the table and acted like I was concerned.

"I think she's had a little too much to drink. I'm going to take her to Silina's house so that I can be sure she makes it home safely. I'm putting you in a cab, Ty. Y'all are in no condition to drive."

It was easier than I'd thought because Ty didn't object. And Tiana was completely out of it, so she didn't have a say so in the matter. I knew that Ty wouldn't think anything of it because she was fucked up and she probably believed that I was really going to take Tiana home. I threw Ty fifty dollars for her cab fare and I picked Tiana up and took her to my truck. When she opened her eyes she was going to be greeted by her worst nightmare.

CHAPTER ELEVEN
Silina

"*Mama!*" I heard London screaming through my house.

I rushed downstairs to where she was at. "Girl, what the hell are you doing screaming through my house like your mind has gone bad? I just put my baby to sleep, and if you wake him up, you're gonna be on baby brother duty. Now what the fuck do you want?"

"Sheesh! Mama, who peed in your Wheaties this morning? I don't want any problems with you, old lady." She cracked a smile and threw her hands up. "I have somebody that I want you to meet. Where is Tiana? She needs to be here too."

"She went out with Ty. I'm glad she is finally getting out the house. So where is this person you want me to meet and who is it?"

"You're about to find out. Tiana! Get your butt down here right now."

I punched her in the arm. "Didn't I just tell your simple ass to stop yelling in my house? I just told you that Tiana ain't here. Why are you still yelling for her?"

"Well, where is she?"

"Have you been listening to anything I just said? Where is your mind? I told you she went out with Ty. Come on, girl. I'm tired so whoever you're trying to introduce me to needs to come on." I stretched and yawned.

London went and opened the door and grabbed somebody's hand. A tall dark skin man walked through my door.

"London, you didn't tell me Morris Chestnut was coming over. I would have done my hair and put on some clothes," I joked.

The young man flashed a beautiful smile that made his already handsome face look even better.

"Mama, this is Elijah, my boyfriend. Elijah this is my mother, Silina."

I reached out to shake his hand and to my surprise he placed a kiss on the back of my hand. "Oh, you must be the man who has my daughter so smitten. It's a pleasure to meet you, Elijah. You must be someone special for my daughter to bring you home."

"It's a pleasure to meet you, Ms. Silina. London speaks very highly of her mother and she was right when she said that she got her looks from you. I would have thought that you were her sister and not her mom."

"You know what they say. Black don't crack. I have been 25 ever since I turned 25. I don't get older. I just get better." We all shared a laugh.

"Excuse me, Mama. Are you flirting with my man?" London joked.

"Chile please! I'm probably old enough to be his mama. I'm no cougar. I need me a sugar daddy." We all laughed at my last statement.

I motioned for Elijah to sit down. "Come have a seat. I wish I would have known that you were coming. I would have cooked dinner. My girls are never home anymore, and my baby boy only drinks formula so I don't cook much nowadays. Maybe next time."

"If London got her cooking skills from you, I'll have to take you up on that offer," Elijah said.

"We're not staying long anyway. I just wanted the two special people in my life to meet Elijah. I wish Tiana was here and Jordan was awake."

"So, Elijah, what do you do? Where are you from? " I questioned.

I played the role of mommy and daddy to London so I was definitely going to drill him. I needed to know everything about this man that my daughter was getting involved with because in my eyes, she was still my baby. I had always been an overprotective mom, and that would never change. You could never be too careful.

"I'm actually from right here in VA, Norfolk that is. I grew up out in Grandy Park, but my dad moved us to Virginia Beach when I was eight. I lived in a house behind South Plaza

Trail and Holland Road all the way up until my pops was killed when I was eighteen. That's when I moved to Maryland, went to school, and opened up my businesses. I own a soul food restaurant in Maryland, and I also own the bar, Paradise, in downtown Norfolk. I have my Associate's degree in business management and I'm working on opening up some more businesses one day."

"I'm so sorry to hear about your dad. I know that he would be proud of the successful young man that you have become. It looks like you've done pretty well for yourself. It's rare to find an educated black man these days, especially one so handsome. London, it looks like you got yourself a keeper."

London's eyes lit up and she was smiling from ear to ear. "Isn't he great?"

"Not half as great as you are," Elijah said right before placing a kiss on her lips.

"I'm glad to see that my daughter is so happy. You better keep it that way, Mr. Elijah because the first time she sheds a tear behind you, you're gonna have to deal with *Mama*." I let him know and I was dead serious.

"You don't have to worry about that. I love to see her smile too much to make her cry. The only tears she'll ever shed because of me are tears of joy. I'm gonna take good care of your daughter."

"I'm sure that you will. It was very nice to meet you, and I hate to be rude, but I need to take a nap before my baby wakes up. Next time you come, we'll sit down and have dinner. Y'all, be safe. I'm going to bed."

"I'll see you later, Ma!"

I walked them out and went back upstairs to get in my bed. As tired as I was, I couldn't fall asleep. My mind drifted off to the four million dollars that was due to hit my account any day from Shawn's life insurance policy. One million was for me and the other three million was to be split equally between the girls.

I hadn't decided what I wanted to do with Milan's portion of the money. I hadn't seen or heard from her in nine months, the day she left my house. She was my daughter so I couldn't help but think about her well being and worry about her. But by the same token, I didn't know if I could ever forgive her. For the life of me, I couldn't figure out why she would want to do something like that to me. I made up my mind to just put her money up for her. It wasn't like I needed it anyway.

Just as I was falling asleep, I heard my doorbell ring. I started to ignore it, but whoever was at my door was very persistent. I saw Jordan moving around in his crib, and he started to whine. I stuck his pacifier in his mouth, and he went right back to sleep. I made a mad dash to the door so the bell wouldn't wake him up.

I swung my door open with much attitude, and on the other side was Patrice.

"Patrice, what the hell are you doing ringing my doorbell like you're crazy? It's ten o'clock at night!"

She walked into my house and started looking around. "Nice house, Silina. You must have yourself a rich husband. I just came to see how you were doing."

Even though it was a cool October night, Patrice had on an ashy black skirt that I was sure would show all of her goodies if she bent over. She had on a pair of run down pumps and a fake ass fur coat that stopped at her waist. Her hair was matted and dirty, and it looked like every tooth in her mouth had decayed. She was toothpick thin, and looked twenty years older than she actually was. The woman looked *bad*! I had heard that she was strung out on drugs. If I didn't believe it before, I damn sure believed it as I eyed her from head to toe. I knew a crack head when I saw one.

"You could have called for that. Cut the bullshit and tell me what you really want."

"Well, I wanted to see if you were able to get the life insurance money. I know my brother left me something." Her eyes jumped around the room while she was talking to avoid making eye contact with me.

"Actually, the only names that were on the policy were my girls and mine. Is there anything you need?"

"That son of a bitch! Yes, there is something I need. I need $100,000."

I laughed out loud when she said that. "Are you serious? I wouldn't dare put $100,000 in your hand for you to blow it all on drugs."

Her eyes got big like her secret was out. She stumbled to find something to say, but nothing came out of her mouth.

"I know you killed my brother, bitch! If you don't give me that money, your ass is going down."

I was shocked that this fiend had the nerve to come up in my crib and disrespect me. I went and stood face to face with her and looked her dead in the eyes. Her eyes were still wandering, and she couldn't keep still.

"No, I didn't kill your brother, but I'm glad he's dead. He wasn't nothing but a psychotic bitch. If I could have pulled the trigger, I would have killed him for all the shit he put me and my family through. Don't you ever bring your funky ass to my house and try to threaten me because I will lay your ass down. Now get the fuck out before I hurt you bitch!"

"This ain't over, Silina. You're going to get yours for what you did. I'm going to get that money one way or another."

"Yeah, over my dead body, and I don't plan on dying before you do. Jump stupid if you want to, and I'll make it look like you overdosed on drugs. Who will give a fuck about a crack head dying?"

Before she could respond I pushed her frail ass out my door and slammed it behind her. "Those drugs must have got the best of that bitch."

I went off to my room and was finally able to go to sleep.

Jordan woke up for his four o'clock bottle. After I fed him, changed his diaper, and put him back to sleep, I got up and walked around my house. It was something I always did to make sure that my daughters had made it home safely. I peeked in London's room and saw that she was sound asleep. I looked in Tiana's room. She wasn't there. I called her phone and didn't get an answer from her. I kept calling, and after the three unanswered calls, I started to get worried.

I ran in London's room, cut the light on, and snatched the cover off of her. "Get up, London *now*!"

She stretched her arms and sat up in the bed. Her eyes weren't able to open all the way because of the light. "What's going on?" she asked.

"Have you talked to Tiana?"

"Not since before her and Ty left to go to the bar. Is something wrong?"

"It's four o'clock in the morning, and Tiana still isn't here. I have been calling her and not getting an answer. It's so unlike her not to come home or at least call if she isn't coming. The bars close at two o'clock. Call Ty and see if you can get an answer from her."

London picked up her phone and on cue it started ringing, displaying a picture of her and Ty. "This is her right here. Hello?"

I couldn't hear what Ty was saying, but whatever it was woke London all the way up. "What the fuck, Ty? Why are you just now calling us? We're on our way!"

"What's wrong? What did she say?" I asked London who had hopped out of bed and was throwing on a pair of black jeans and a black hoodie.

"She said that she and Tiana were drunk, and Chief was at the bar. He offered to bring Tiana here, and he told Ty to catch a cab. She was calling me to make sure Tiana made it home. I know that he has Tiana. We have to find out where he is!"

I couldn't believe this shit. Chief had been smiling in my face trying his hardest to get us back together when he had been plotting on my daughter the whole time. Too many people had fucked me over this year, but that was about to come to an end. I had it set in my mind that Chief was going to die that night. I told my daughter I would kill him before I let anything else happen to her, and that's exactly what the fuck I meant.

I heard London on the phone talking to someone as I was trying to collect my thoughts. I didn't know what to do next because I had Jordan to think about and I couldn't just leave him. I started blowing Chief's phone up, but it was going straight to voicemail. I went into panic mode instantly.

"Mama, Elijah is on his way to pick us up right now. Ty is going to come over here and sit with Jordan, and we're going to handle this shit. In the meantime, I need you to use your phone to locate Tiana. We all have 'find my iPhone' enabled, so we will be able to see where her phone is. That should take us right to her."

I used my phone to try to track down Tiana. Her phone was somewhere in Suffolk. I didn't waste anytime getting dressed in all black and putting my pistol in my hip holster. After all the events that had transpired this year, I thought it would be best to have a gun. I had to be the one to protect my family because I was all they had. I knew the night air was cold, so I threw on a black leather jacket to hide my gun.

Elijah and Ty got there in record time, and London and I damn near fell over each other trying to get out of the door. I told Ty where to find everything she needed for the baby and within a few seconds we had jumped in Elijah's car and were flying down the road. The whole way there, I was praying that we weren't too late. I had almost lost my baby girl once and I didn't want to think about it happening again.

When we arrived at the destination that the GPS had directed us to, Elijah shut the headlights off and parked up the block. We were out in the country, and it looked like some type of cabin.

I heard Elijah tell London to stay in the car and lookout for anyone. I hopped out of the car and moved swiftly up the street to get to the house. I knew we were at the right place because I saw Chief's truck parked outside. Elijah caught up with me and told me to go knock on the front door to catch Chief off guard. He was going to find another way in so he could surprise him.

When I made it to the front door I twisted the knob to see if it was open, but it wasn't so I banged on the door. It didn't take any time for Chief to see who was banging on his door in the wee hours of the morning.

"What the fuck? Silina?" He looked like a kid caught with his hand in the cookie jar when he saw me standing on his front porch. "What are you doing here this time of night? Is my son okay?"

I pulled the gun out of my holster and pointed it right in his face. "After today, you will probably never see your son again. Get your ass inside this fuckin' house!" I knew I had an advantage because he didn't have a weapon on him at the moment. "Put your fuckin' hands up, bitch!"

His hands shot in the air instantly. "What the fuck are you doing waving a gun in my face? What the fuck is this about?"

"You know exactly what this is about. Where the fuck is my daughter?" My eyes scanned the living room and the kitchen and I saw no sign of her.

"I don't know what you're talking about."

"You know exactly what the fuck I'm talking about. Ty told me all about what happened."

When I mentioned Ty, there was guilt written all over his face. All of a sudden I heard noises coming from upstairs. I started going toward where I heard the sound coming from because I knew that it was Tiana. When I went into the bedroom I didn't see Tiana, but I saw another door. I rushed over to the door and as soon as I went to turn the knob, Chief grabbed the hood of my coat and flung me to the floor.

CHAPTER TWELVE
Elijah

The cat and mouse game I was playing with Chief was finally about to come to an end, and he didn't even know it. After deciding to just wait for the right moment, the perfect opportunity had finally presented itself just like I knew it would. Instead of having to waste time going out and looking for him, he had set himself up.

When Silina went and knocked on the door I went around to the back of the house and saw an open window. I pulled myself up on the roof and climbed to the second floor. I looked in the window before I went in and I saw Chief throw Silina to the ground. Her gun flew out of her hand and that's when I made my move.

I came through the window so fast that I took both of them by surprise. Chief looked at me like he was seeing a ghost. I felt my blood boiling. I was so enraged that I started sweating. Chief had a smirk on his face while he stared at me. He tried to grab Silina's gun.

He moved fast, but not faster than I did. Instead of getting to the gun he ran into my fist instead.

I never looked up or stopped fighting, but I told Silina, "Get your gun and go find your daughter. Take her to the car and wait for me."

She ran off and opened the door that she was trying to get in before. I continued to beat Chief's face into a bloody pulp with my bare hands. He was fighting back, but that was a match that he didn't stand a chance in hell of winning. No matter how hard or how many times I hit that motherfucker, he wouldn't even stumble. The nigga was putting up a good fight. He got me a couple of times and when he did catch me, it showed. My lip was busted and my nose was bleeding. That didn't compare to the blows he was taking. A lot of niggas needed a gun, but I could kill a nigga with just my hands if need be. I made my last hit count when I knocked a couple of teeth out his mouth and dropped him right where he stood.

I watched Silina trying to help her daughter who could barely walk on her own. She picked her up and carried her out of the room, and I thought to myself, *damn she's a strong woman.*

"So you're the bitch ass nigga who killed my pops, huh?"

Chief was still disoriented from the blows he'd taken, but he was still the same shit talking ass nigga. "You damn right I had your daddy killed. What the fuck you gonna do about it, youngin'? I almost killed your bitch ass too. You just got lucky. That nigga, Big John, thought that he couldn't be knocked off that high horse he was on, but I proved him wrong." He started laughing hysterically.

I didn't have any more time to waste, and I was never a man of many words when it came to handling my business. I pulled out my gun and emptied the clip into that motherfucker. As I filled his body with lead, I felt a satisfaction that I hadn't felt in a while. I had finally avenged my father's death and I knew that I would sleep better at night because of it.

CHAPTER THIRTEEN
London

Three months had passed since Elijah killed Chief in that cabin, and nobody lost any sleep behind it. Even my mom, who I thought would be distraught about losing her husband, seemed to be taking it pretty well. I noticed more of a difference in Elijah than anyone else. It seemed like he was more at peace knowing that he avenged his father's death. He no longer had to look over his shoulder and wonder if he was going to get got first. The only thing on his mind now was me and our baby and he made sure he catered to me in every way all throughout my pregnancy.

When I told everybody the news about me being pregnant they were ecstatic. I found out that I was having a girl and they couldn't wait to start shopping. Between Mama, Tiana, Aunt Precious, and Ty our baby already had a full wardrobe from newborn sizes all the way up to twelve months and I was only six months pregnant.

I heard the doorbell ring but I couldn't get up fast enough to get it. My mom got to the door before I did and when she opened it Elijah walked in.

"How you doing Ms. Silina," he asked. He then hugged her and gave her a kiss on the cheek.

"I'm doing just fine, how about you?"

"I can't complain. I had to come check on my ladies. What's that I smell cooking up in here?"

"I'm making some fried chicken, ribs, baked macaroni and cheese, homemade collard greens, candied yams, and some cornbread."

"You throwing down in the kitchen Ms. Silina, let me find out! Sound like I'ma be staying for dinner," Elijah said.

"You know you're more than welcome to. Let me get back in this kitchen before dinner gets served Cajun style," she joked and went back into the kitchen.

Elijah walked over to the couch I was sitting on and kissed me while rubbing on my stomach. He leaned down and placed soft kisses on my stomach too.

"I got something I want to show you baby mama," Elijah joked. He knew I hated that term and he always taunted me.

"I got your damn baby mama. What you got to show me?" I asked curiously. It was no telling with Elijah because he was full of surprises.

"I'll only show you if you let me blindfold you," he smirked.

A mischievous grin spread across my face. "What type of freaky shit you got going on?"

"Just trust me," he said before he kissed me with those juicy lips.

He sat me back down in the chair and stood behind me. He covered my eyes with a silk blindfold and I heard him walk out the room. When he came back I felt him lift my foot up and put a sneaker on it. He did the same thing for my other foot. That one small gesture meant so much to me because he knew how hard it was for me to put on shoes with the size of my stomach. I had gained forty pounds and it showed. It was the little things like that that made me love him even more.

He placed a strong hand on my lower back and used the other hand to grab my hand and help me up out of the chair. I didn't know where we were going but I followed his lead and he guided me along the way. He put my coat on for me and wrapped a scarf around my neck. I could tell when we went outside because even though I was bundled up, the cold winter air still stung my face. He guided me to the car and gently helped me in and closed my door.

As soon I heard him get in I bombarded him with questions. "What's going on? Where are you taking me? Can you tell me what you gotta show me? Or at least give me a hint."

I heard him start snickering. "Chill! Just sit back and relax. You'll see it when we get there. Don't keep asking me questions girl!" With that he cut the radio up and we listened to Young Jeezy for the rest of the ride.

We finally came to a stop and he got out and opened my door. Anticipation was killing me. I couldn't wait to see what Elijah had in store for me. He slid his arm around my waist and we walked up three steps. We walked a little further and next thing I know I was waddling up a whole flight of stairs.

"What type of surprise requires this much walking?" I asked, out of breathe. "Shit! All this exercise is making me hungry."

Elijah shut me up by taking the blindfold off of my eyes. I looked around and I was standing in the middle of a huge room. The walls were painted a soft pink and there was a white crib, two white dressers, and a white rocking chair. There was even a little white rocking horse. The carpet in the room was also pink. On the wall above the crib there was a pair of ballet slippers painted there. The top of the dresser was stocked up with wipes, body wash, lotion, and powder. The open closet door revealed a closet full of little baby clothes and shoes. In the corner sat cases of diapers and wipes.

"This is a beautiful nursery. Whose house is this?"

Elijah smiled from ear to ear. "It's yours," he said and handed me a key that he had pulled out of his pocket.

"Aaaahhh!! Oh my God! No you didn't buy me a house Elijah!" I ran over to him and gave him a hug but my big belly stopped me from grabbing him like I wanted to. I wrapped my arm around his neck, pulled him down to my level, and kissed him passionately.

Tears started freely flowing down my face. Elijah never ceased to amaze me. For a moment I just looked him in his eyes and then I kissed him slowly again.

"You don't know how much I appreciate you and everything you do to make my life better. I can't believe you bought me a house! Thank you so much! I gotta call Mama and them!" I was so excited I couldn't hide the smile on my face even if I wanted to.

"You don't have to thank me. I'm just a man who handles his business. You didn't think I was going to have you and my baby living with your mom forever did you? Why don't you go check out the rest of the house?"

He didn't have to tell me twice. I moved as fast as my body would let me and went back down the stairs to start there. Elijah was right behind me, making sure I didn't bust my ass.

"I thought you would like to decorate the rest of the house yourself. I wanted to do the baby girl's room personally, but you can always add on," Elijah announced.

"It's beautiful just how it is. I love it. And I love you," I gushed.

When I reached the bottom of the stairs I noticed that the front door to the house was huge. It had a window on each side of it that went from the floor to the high ceiling. From the front door you could look up and see the upstairs balcony. The spiral staircase was the first thing you saw when you entered the house. On the right of the stairs there was a massive living room. There were two big windows in the living room and I loved windows because I needed sunlight. Even though the house was empty I was amazed at how spacious the place was.

I walked further down the hallway and walked into a big kitchen. I noticed there were two entrances in the kitchen. There was an island in the middle with black marble countertops and black appliances. A microwave hung over the stove and even the refrigerator was black. To the left of the kitchen was a den that was almost just as big as the living room. It had French doors that led to what I assumed was a back yard. I decided I would look at that last and check out the rest of the house.

To the right of the kitchen was a dining room. A chandelier hung from the ceiling. I was more than impressed with what I saw already. I walked back upstairs and saw that there were four bedrooms. The master bedroom was at the end of the hall so I went there first. I fell in love with the closet as soon as I saw it. It was just what I needed for all the shit I had. The closet was big enough to fit a bed and dresser in there. There was a patio door in the room and I walked outside to see what it was like. The door led to a balcony that overlooked the lake at the city park Mt. Trashmore. From the balcony I saw how big the back yard was. There was a deck back there and also a gazebo. I could put a whole park back there if I wanted to.

I felt Elijah come put his arms around my belly from behind and pull me close to him. "I can't wait to wake up to that beautiful face every morning. I'll rent a truck and help you move your stuff in tomorrow." He kissed me on the back of my neck and I could feel his dick getting hard.

"Okay, I can't wait to start decorating. But first let's break this house in," I grinned.

That was exactly what we did, in every single room of the house, except our baby's room. I felt like I was walking on clouds. No man had ever made me as happy as Elijah did. He treated me like the queen that he knew I was, and he was definitely my king.

Elijah

3 months later

"I told you that you were having my baby girl, didn't I?"

"Yes, you did, and we made a beautiful baby girl. Look at all this pretty curly hair. She gets that from you," London said.

She was holding our daughter close to her chest like she was the most precious gift in the world, and to us she was. Watching London have my baby made me fall in love like I had never been before. When my daughter and I made eye contact, I knew that there was nothing in the world she couldn't get from me if she asked for it. That little girl stole my heart. She was my princess.

"I finally got the family I had always dreamed about. I wish my dad was here to share the moment with me," I admitted. It was bittersweet for me just for that reason right there.

"He is here to share it with you right here, baby." London pointed to my heart. "He's always in your heart and on your mind, so there's never a time that he's not with you. Your dad is looking down on you smiling from ear to ear at the man he raised." She leaned over and kissed me on the cheek.

I looked over at Silina. She was shedding tears. "This is such a beautiful moment. For the first time in a while, we're finally all happy. What are you going to name my grandbaby?"

"We're going to name her Ariana Navaeh."

"That's beautiful. She and her uncle are going to grow up more like brother and sister."

"They sure are. And you know Jordan is going to think he runs that," Tiana said and laughed. "That's good, though. I always wished I had an older brother to protect me. I have my bro, Elijah, now so I guess my wish came true." She looked at me and smiled.

"So what, your big sister didn't protect you enough?" London joked.

"I didn't say that. It's nothing like having a big brother though," Tiana countered.

There was a genuine love between me and this family, and I was glad that I had made the choice to be with London. I truly loved her and she loved me for who I was and not for what I had. I had never been happier in my life and I wanted it to stay that way. I had made the decision to get out of the game when my daughter was born, and that was exactly what I was going to do after I tied up a few loose ends. I had more than enough money to sit back and chill.

Tiana got up and walked over to London. "Give me my niece. Y'all being stingy with her already," she joked while gently taking Ariana out of her arms.

"Ms. Silina, can I talk to you in private for a minute?"

"Sure. Let's go down to the café. Anybody want something while we're down there?"

"Nope. I'm fine," London said.

"I want a Pepsi," Tiana answered.

I opened the door for her to leave the hospital room and I walked out behind her.

"I'm so happy for you and London. I never thought I would see this day come. I can't believe I'm a grandma. That baby is going to be spoiled rotten." Silina said.

"Indeed she is. I pulled you to the side because after all this time I never got to apologize."

Silina got a confused look on her face. "Apologize for what?"

"For killing the father of your baby. I'm not sorry for what I did to him, but I'm sorry for not giving you a choice but to be a single mother. I know how it feels to know that somebody murdered your dad, and even though Chief deserved what he got, Jordan didn't. I want you to know that I will be there for Jordan in every way possible. He won't have to miss out on a father figure because big bro will show him the way. If there's anything I can do, please let me know and I mean that. I love all of y'all and I will do anything for you."

"That really means a lot to me, Elijah. Jordan already loves you and you're a great man for him to look up to. Thank you, son. We love you too. You have already proven your loyalty to us."

"There's one more thing I wanted to talk to you about," I added.

"What's that?"

"I want to ask London to marry me."

"Aaaah! Oh my God! Oh my God! My baby is getting married!"

"Could you keep this between you and me please? I wanted to get your approval before I just popped the question."

"You know you have my approval, boy! When do you plan on proposing?"

"I'm not sure of an exact day, but some time soon. I'm thinking about doing it on her birthday."

"June 12th? That's two months away. I can't wait to see the look on her face. If I'm this ecstatic, can you imagine how happy this is going to make her?"

"That's the only thing I want to do for the rest of her life. I just want to make her happy. She has made me a very happy man."

"Well, you know you have my blessing. Let me know if you need help with anything."

"You know I will."

After Silina got what she wanted from the café, we walked back up to the room to be with London and Ariana. My girls were the most important things to me, and I was going to make our family official.

CHAPTER FOURTEEN
Silina

The blessings that my family had been receiving were nothing short of amazing. Tiana was a strong young lady because even after being shot and then drugged and kidnapped, she didn't let anything get her down. She didn't dwell on the past. Shooting toward her future goals was what had kept her going. Both of my girls were still excelling in school, and I was so proud.

London had just had a baby and she was in a happy relationship with Elijah. He had just told me that he was going to propose to her, and I couldn't have been any happier for her. I had recently opened up another boutique in LA with the money I'd received from Shawn's life insurance. All four of my boutiques were thriving, and the most I had to do was go check in on them from time to time. I had the best staff working in all of them. I let Precious run the one here in VA and I paid her a nice salary.

My girls were trying to get me to date again, but I wasn't ready for all that just yet. The previous two men had wreaked havoc on my life and my children's, and I had vowed to never let a man be my downfall again. It was crazy how people could put on a mask and be a totally different person. That just goes to show how you couldn't trust people.

When both of my daughters decided to move out on their own, I sold our house and moved into a condo in the Town Center section of Virginia Beach. There was no need for Jordan and me to live in that big house. Besides, it brought back too many memories that I wanted to forget.

My phone rung and snapped me out of my thoughts. I didn't recognize the number.

"Hello?"

"Hi, Silina, this is Dr. Weiss. Do you have a minute?"

"How are you doctor? Yes, I have a minute, especially if this call is concerning my health. Is everything all right?"

"Actually, this call isn't concerning you at all. It's about your daughter, Milan."

I hadn't heard Milan's name in so long that it caught me completely off guard. "What about her?"

"I was the only doctor on call at the hospital today and I had a patient that is in a coma, but her baby was still growing inside of her. They asked me to deliver the child by C-section. When I saw who the patient was, I couldn't believe it."

"I don't mean to cut you off, but what does this have to do with Milan or me?"

"Silina, the patient was *Milan*. You're a grandmother now, and the baby has nowhere to go. I'm not sure who the father is, but Milan still hasn't come out of her coma. I called you because I knew that you would want to take your grandson until Milan gets better."

I couldn't believe the words that had come out of her mouth. I didn't know anything about what had gone on with Milan over the past year, so I was completely in the blind. I happened to already be in the hospital, so I went to the information desk and asked where Milan was. Once I was given her room number, I went straight there.

My daughter was lying in a hospital bed looking lifeless. She was hooked up to all types of machines and had a tube running down her throat. Seeing my daughter in this predicament and not knowing how she had ended up there was a huge blow to my heart. I instantly started crying and ran to her side.

"What happen to you, Milan? I don't know if you can hear me, but I forgive you. I never stopped loving you and I want you to get better," I cried.

I couldn't believe that my daughter was in a coma and I knew nothing about it. I was harboring a whole lot of resentment toward her and I hadn't been there for her when she'd needed me the most. If she didn't make it out of this, I would never forgive myself.

I heard the door to the room open and I looked up to see a doctor walk in. "What happened to my daughter? I'm her mother, Silina."

"Hi, Silina, I'm Dr. Jackson. You daughter was brought here in very critical condition. She was repeatedly beaten in the head with a blunt object and left for dead in the woods in Northern Virginia. Someone happened to find her there and called for help. She was at a hospital there and the only way she could be identified was by dental records. The hospital had her transferred over here once they found out who she was so that it would be easier for her family to find her. Your daughter is in a vegetative state, but miraculously her baby developed normally."

I thought that I was going to lose my breath. "Did they find the person that did this to my baby? How long ago did this happen?"

"You'll have to contact the police department, but she has been here for six months."

If I wasn't already sitting down I would have collapsed. "How long will she be in this state?"

"Right now the only thing we can do is wait it out."

"So where is the baby?" I asked.

"He's down in the nursery. You're welcome to go see him. We're going to need someone to be his legal guardian or we are going to have to send him to foster care. Do you know anything about the father?"

"No, I don't, but I'll be taking my grandbaby home with me. Can you show me where to find him?"

The doctor took me to the nursery and showed me which bassinet my grandbaby was in. He left me alone to get a private moment with my grandson. I looked inside the bassinet and saw a tiny sleeping baby. My heart instantly filled with joy. Ironically, both of my twins had given birth to babies on the same day. I couldn't help but wonder who the father of my grandson was and where he was at.

I picked him up and as soon as he was in my arms, his little eyes open. The more I stared into his eyes the more familiar he started to look to me.

"Ain't this a bitch!" I yelled, waking up some of the babies, causing them all to cry simultaneously.

I put my grandson back in his bassinet and ran out of the room in a hurry. I flew to London's hospital room and tried to calm myself down before I went inside. I went in with a smile on my face and acted like everything was cool. London and Elijah looked so happy and engrossed with their beautiful baby girl that I'm not even sure if they noticed me come in the room.

"Tiana can I speak to you for a second," I whispered in her ear so I wouldn't alarm anyone.

Without any hesitation Tiana got up and followed me out the door. As soon as the door shut I grabbed her hand and flew down the hall once again. Tiana didn't have a choice but to keep up because I never let go of her hand.

"What's going on mama?" she asked but I just kept right on running.

When we finally made it to the nursery Tiana was out of breathe and still had no idea what was going on.

"Can you tell me what's wrong with you mama? You're scaring me acting all weird and stuff."

"Look at this baby right here. Tell me who you think he looks like."

"Awwww he looks just like Jordan did when he was born. What's your point?"

"This is Milan's son."

Tiana's eyes grew wide with shock and her mouth dropped open so wide that I thought a fly was going to go down her throat.

"So Milan is in the hospital? She had a baby and didn't tell anybody?"

"She didn't tell anybody because she couldn't. She is in a coma and has been in one for six months. Somebody beat her in the head with something and left her for dead in the woods…"

In the middle of me explaining the situation at hand Tiana looked like she wanted to faint. "WH-what? Who would do that to my sister? Is she going to be ok?"

"I don't know what's going to happen to her. I'm praying that she does pull through. This baby needs his mother. That's not my point though. Take a closer look at this baby and tell me what you think."

Tiana slowly picked up her nephew and he started to cry. She gently rocked him and hummed a lullaby in his ear. Whatever she was doing was soothing to him because he stopped crying just as quickly as he started. Tiana took her time and actually examined the baby boy that she was cradling in her arms.

"Mama you're not saying that this is Chief's baby...are you?"

"That's exactly what the fuck I'm saying. I don't know for sure but it's too close for my comfort. Jordan and this baby are damn near twins! If that's the case that means that they were still fucking!"

"This is too much for me. I mean seriously this family needs a reality show! Where is my sister? Do you think that Chief is the one who did this to her because he didn't want you to find out about her pregnancy?"

"I don't know what the fuck happened. We may never know with Chief being dead and Milan being in a coma. What

I do know is that I'm getting a blood test on this baby. I have to know the truth!"

Just that quickly my world had turned upside down once again and I was facing the same situation that broke me over a year ago. Chief was still fucking with me from the grave and Milan apparently didn't give a fuck that she lost everything behind that man. She didn't learn anything at all because she was still fucking him. I didn't know what to do anymore and I was starting to wonder if someone put a curse on my damn life.

CHAPTER FIFTEEN
London

I had never had this much happiness at one time in my entire life. I had the man of my dreams by my side, I had a gorgeous baby girl by him, and we had more than enough money to take care of ourselves for three lifetimes. Elijah told me that he was leaving the game alone and focusing on his family and his businesses. He didn't want his daughter to have a dope dealing father and he told me that I deserved more than the street life. I was less than a year away from getting my masters degree. I literally felt like I was floating on a cloud. The only thing that was missing was a ring.

"Everything good with you baby?" Elijah's deep voice interrupted my thoughts.

"I'm good boo, just thinking about how happy I am. You and Ariana are my world and I don't believe it can get any better than this."

"Oh it can get way better than this, and it will. One day we'll have a house full of kids running around," he smiled.

After all that time his smile still made me melt. "Slow your roll now buddy! I just went through twelve hours of hard labor to push this one out. Let's give her the world before we decide to have more." I laughed.

I honestly couldn't wait to have more of his babies, of course after he decided he wanted to make me his wife.

"I have someone I want you to meet," Elijah said as he got up to open the door to the hospital room.

Behind the door was a lady that had to be in her mid to late forties. Her hair was pulled back into a bun and there were tiny pieces of gray in the front. For an older woman she was in great shape and I could tell that she was a force to be reckoned with back in the day. She was a beautiful dark skin lady and it wasn't long before I noticed the resemblance between her and Elijah.

"London, I would like you to meet my mother Angela. Ma this is the mother of my daughter and the love of my life." Elijah introduced us.

Angela didn't say anything immediately but I could see tears starting to form in her eyes when she looked at me and a sleeping Ariana.

"Y'all know holding that baby while she is sleep ain't gonna do nothing but spoil her to death. Now give me my grandbaby," she nearly ran to our side and took the baby out of my arms. As soon as she had her in her hands she burst out in full blown tears.

"I'm sorry for being so rude London. It's very nice to meet you. I'm happy to know that my son found someone to have his own family with. You have an amazing man on your hands so you take care of him," she said through tears.

What I wanted to say was, you should have been the one taking care of him instead of running off on him for a piece of dick but instead I said, "Nice to meet you too Ms. Angela.

Don't worry; I will take good care of this family. I know what I have and I'm going to cherish it for the rest of my life."

As if she read my thoughts she replied, "I know I haven't been the best mother to you Elijah. I was young and I made so many mistakes but if you are willing to let me I plan on fixing them all. I want to be in my granddaughter's life and make up for all the lost time with you Elijah."

"I forgive you ma. Let's not talk about all of that right now. I just want to enjoy having the ladies in my life all together for the first time. We're only missing Ms. Silina and Tiana. Where are they anyway? I noticed that they left the room in a hurry but I didn't want to get all up in their business so I just let them be. Have you heard from them?"

"No I haven't but I'm about to call. I know they would love to meet you Angela."

As I was dialing Tiana's number they came back in the room. They were trying to look like everything was cool but I knew them like the back of my hand so I knew something was up. I gave them both a look to let them know I was on to them but I wasn't going to say anything right then.

"I was just about to call y'all. I want to introduce you to Elijah's mom, Angela. Ms. Angela this is my mother Silina and my little sister Tiana."

They all gave each other hugs and made small talk. Elijah knew me so well that he knew I was itching to see what the fuck was going on, so he told his mom that he was going to pick us up something to eat and he wanted her to join him.

As soon as they were out of the room I started drilling my family. "Y'all care to tell me what had y'all running out of the room in such a hurry without telling me anything?" I asked with an eyebrow raised in suspicion.

"We don't want to ruin this joyous occasion with drama so let's just save it for a later date," my mom answered.

I ignored her and looked over at Tiana. She was standing there looking like she didn't know whether to tell me or keep her mouth shut.

"Just tell me what's going on please, don't let my mind wander because that will only make things worse."

"Milan is in this hospital right now in a coma. She's been in one for six months now," Tiana blurted.

My mom gave her the look of death and I knew she wanted to smack the shit out of Tiana for going against what she had already said.

"Doesn't sound like such bad news to me," I shrugged.

I didn't know why I still harbored so much resentment towards Milan. Her and her little boyfriend caused so much strife to this family that I didn't think I could ever forgive her. If she had never started fucking Chief in the first place, a lot of the shit this family went through could have been avoided.

"That's your fuckin twin sister you're talking about London!" my mom snapped.

"She's also the same bitch that was fuckin your husband for two years so don't be so quick to defend her!" I responded.

With lightning speed my mama slapped me so hard that I immediately rubbed my face to try to relieve the stinging sensation. I didn't even see the shit coming so I was completely caught off guard.

"Watch how the fuck you talk to me. Have some fuckin respect you little bitch!" she stormed out of the room, leaving me and Tiana standing there speechless.

"You deserved that shit London. I mean what the fuck were you thinking?"

"The shit is fuckin true!! I cut that bitch off for her and this is what I get in return. This is some fuckin bullshit. Show your loyalty for motherfuckers and they will show you how they really feel. Where the fuck did she come from trying to defend Milan all of a sudden?"

"Have you ever thought that maybe she let go of the shit and forgave her? It didn't sound like she was defending her to me. It sounds like you have some shit that you need to let go of because mama is right, that is your sister."

"I don't know what the fuck is wrong with y'all but y'all are on some bullshit!"

"You will feel a whole lot better if you just forgive and forget. It takes way more energy to hate someone than it does to just let karma deal with them," Tiana said.

"Well it looks like karma is dealing with her ass now but y'all want to run to her side like some little bitches! Where the fuck was she when you were in the hospital after getting shot? Did she come to your side to see if you were going to live or die? Hell no! What about when she thought it was ok to fuck Chief. Did she think about how she would affect everybody around her by doing that triflin ass shit? Hell fuckin no! I see that y'all just don't know when enough is enough. Before I give that bitch a chance to do me or anyone around me dirty again I will kill her myself."

Tiana looked at me and shook her head. "Who are you London? What has gotten into you? Yes Milan has been a very fucked up individual. I can't disagree with you on that. But damn your twin sister may not even make it and you just can't let the shit go. You need some fuckin help because apparently your hate for Milan has consumed you and that's a fuckin problem. We have a nephew that we have to worry about and all you can do is...."

"Wait what?" I cut Tiana off. "What do you mean we have a nephew?"

"What the fuck do you think I mean? Milan had a baby. Isn't it ironic y'all were born on the same day now your kids share a birthday?"

I couldn't even find any words to say. As much as I didn't like my twin I still wanted to meet my nephew. "Well where is he?"

"He's in the nursery right now. Mama is going to take care of him until Milan gets better. The crazy part about the whole thing is we think that her baby is Chief's. That little boy looks identical to Jordan!"

I looked at Tiana to make sure that I heard correctly. "What the fuck? Damn when will the madness ever stop?"

"I don't know but mama is going to get a blood test on him."

"I think she should just leave it alone because if she finds out it is Chief's baby that will only make shit more complicated."

"Yeah well why don't you try telling her that? You see where running that mouth got you earlier. Just let her do what she do. You do know that we have to help her out though right? I know that you just had a baby and you have a lot on your plate right now but our nephew doesn't have a mother right now so we have to come together and make sure that he is taken care of."

I just nodded my head at her. "Yeah I know. The baby didn't ask to be here and no matter what I will always love my nephew. I can't wait to see him!" I gushed.

"You're going to fall in love the same way I fell in love with him and Ariana. As a matter of fact I'm about to wake my niece up so she can bond with her auntie. Why don't you go ahead to the nursery and see the baby."

I agreed to go see my nephew. I got up out the hospital bed and slid my feet in a pair of flip flops. I was looking rough with a pair of oversized sweat pants and a white t-shirt on but I didn't care. As I was walking down the hall I ran into Elijah and Angela coming back to the room with pizzas.

"Where you headed to?" Elijah asked.

I gave him a look to tell him that it was personal and he sent his mom back to the room so we could get some privacy. I gave Elijah the rundown of what was going on and he was at a loss for words.

"I guess bodying that nigga wasn't enough because he is still making Ms. Silina's life miserable as fuck," he shook his head. "Come on I'll go with you to see the baby."

We walked into the nursery and the nurse didn't even check the wrist bands the doctor gave us to have access to the nursery. I made a mental note to not let my baby go back in that nursery again because that was careless. If we were crazy we could have walked out of there with anyone's baby without them knowing.

My eyes scanned the room and I instantly found my nephew. His eyes were wide open and he was looking right at me. As soon as I laid eyes on him I fell in love, just like Tiana said I would. I picked him up and started talking baby talk to him.

"Damn they didn't lie when they said him and Jordan were identical. This is exactly how Jordan looked when he was born! You see I wasn't lying when I told you what type of bitch Milan was! Don't worry little baby, auntie got you. Your grandma, your other aunt, and I are going to take good care of you." I said to the baby.

I looked up to see that Elijah was looking at me with a smile on his face. "What are you smiling about?" I wondered.

"Just because I love you and I admire the woman you are. There are bitches out here who would say fuck that baby just because of the history y'all have with Milan but y'all are stepping up. That's what family is supposed to do. I knew that I never had to doubt your loyalty but you keep proving that to me everyday."

"At the end of the day that is my sister and my nephew. I'm probably the closest thing to his mother since we are twins. Even though I highly doubt that Milan would do it for me I would never leave my nephew outback with nowhere to go and no one to turn to."

Elijah didn't say anything else. He just placed a kiss on my lips and gently took the baby out of my arms. He was so good with kids and I couldn't have asked for a better father for my baby. We spent a few more minutes bonding with my nephew before I started missing my own daughter and had to get back to her. After I saw the baby, things didn't seem so bad anymore. Even though the baby belonged to Milan and possibly Chief, we had another bundle of joy to add to our family. It didn't matter who his parents were, he was just as much a part of us as the rest of the family.

CHAPTER SIXTEEN
London

"Waaahhh!! Waaahhh!! Waaahhh!!"

"Girl I don't see how your mama had twins 'cause I wouldn't be able to do it. Two babies crying at the same damn time and not knowing what the fuck is wrong with them gotta be stressful," Ty said as she walked over to the crib and picked up Caiden, which my mom named Milan's son.

I grabbed Ariana out of her crib and walked around the room with pale pink walls with her in my arms. I had both of the babies and when I had them together it was exactly like having twins. I loved it though and didn't have any complaints. Elijah helped me tremendously with both of them when Caiden was here. He wasn't like the average nigga that would leave all the responsibility on the mom. When we came home from the hospital he got up in the middle of the night, changed diapers, and made bottles. He was there for me just like he had been throughout my entire pregnancy. For the first week of Ariana's life we all stayed locked up in the two story, four bedroom house that he bought us in Virginia Beach. He catered to me like the queen that I was and did everything for his daughter by himself.

"I know what's wrong with them, it's time for them to be fed and changed. Since you're here you might as well be useful and help a sister out. I got her can you get him for me please?"

"I got you girl. I'm going to change both of them while you make the bottles."

Ty had been a big help to me too after I had the baby. When it was my time to have Caiden she would come over and help me out if she knew Elijah wasn't going to be around. One thing Caiden didn't lack was love. Between me, my mom, Tiana, and Elijah he was well taken care of. He had his own room at all of our houses full of clothes, pampers, wipes, a crib, and anything else you could think of that a baby needs.

I finished the bottles and handed one to Ty as I picked up Caiden and fed him. By the time Ariana and Caiden were finished eating they were both sound asleep. We put them in their cribs and turned the baby monitors on. Ty went and got two wine glasses from the kitchen and poured us some Moscato.

"Somebody's about to be 25 tomorrow, I'll drink to that. I wish you had something stronger than this weak ass bullshit," Ty laughed. "I can't wait to turn up tomorrow at your party. You know it's gonna be like that!"

"I know I can't wait either! The only thing I'm not ready for is leaving my baby girl. I feel like it's too soon."

"Girl please, celebrate your birthday! It's normal to feel the way you do about leaving Ariana but she is going to be in good hands. It's only a few hours and you deserve to get out and have some fun. It felt like your ass was pregnant for a whole damn year and now it's time for you to celebrate!"

"I guess you're right. I do need to get my sexy on and shut the city down like old times," I slapped Ty a high five. "Elijah is going to have the babies tomorrow so I can go out and get pampered and ready for my party. You wanna come with?"

"Hell yeah you know I'm down. It's on me birthday girl. Let me go home and get some rest so I can be prepared for this long day. You need to get some sleep too while the kids are sleeping because you know they're gonna be hollering soon."

"Make sure you get your shit off my table before you leave bitch!" I said. Ty picked up the wine glasses and took them in the kitchen.

I walked her to the front door and watched her until she got in the car and pulled off. I saw the headlights to Elijah's black on black Porsche pulling up as I was closing the door. I waited in the doorway for him to get out of the car and come in the house. He was looking good in all black with Gucci shoes and a matching belt on. He grabbed me by my waist and pulled me close to his body. He kissed me and used his tongue to separate my lips. Our tongues did a tango as I got lost in the passionate kiss. After all this time sparks still flew every time he touched or kissed me. He tore his lips away from mine and stepped inside the house.

"The babies must be sleep for the house to be this quiet," he said.

"You know it! Ty just left; she helped me get them to sleep."

"Good now we can bring your birthday in the right way," he smirked while pulling a bottle of peach Patron out of a black plastic bag.

A smile crept up on my face. I already knew what time it was when the liquor started flowing.

"Why don't you go upstairs and freshen up. I'll be down here waiting on you."

I didn't know what is was but I knew that Elijah had something up his sleeve. I went up the stairs and went in the huge master bedroom. I went in the bathroom which was equipped with his and hers sinks on a marble countertop, a Jacuzzi tub and a walk in shower. As I was removing my clothes I glanced at myself in the mirror. After having Ariana my body looked better than it ever had before. I lost my stomach almost instantly and the baby phat went to other places. I got thicker in all the right places. Elijah loved the way my hips and thighs spread and my ass poked out. I went from a size 9 to a 13 but it was a smooth transition and I loved it.

I relaxed and soaked in the Jacuzzi for a little while then went to go sit on my bed and air dry by the fan like I always did. To my surprise when I walked out of the bathroom Tiana was sitting on my bed.

"Bitch you scared the shit out of me! What the fuck are you doing popping up in my room unannounced anyway?"

"I came to help out with the kids so you can enjoy your birthday. Just get your life together and carry your ass back downstairs to your man," Tiana said.

I brushed my hair up into a high bun and threw on some midi shorts and a camisole. I went to the stairs and noticed that a candle was lit on each step. When I got to the bottom of the stairs HAPPY BIRTHDAY was spelled out in tea light candles in the foyer. I snatched my phone out of my pocket and took a picture of the beautiful set up from every angle.

I still didn't see Elijah so I walked in the living room and on the table were bouquets of flowers. There were two dozen white roses, two dozen red roses, and a dozen yellow roses. Each single flower was wrapped in hundred dollar bills. There was also a bouquet of Victoria's Secret panties along with various lotions and perfumes. My smile got wider and wider as I ran through the house in excitement looking for Elijah. When I went to the kitchen I found shopping bags filled with jewelry, clothes and shoes. I was like a kid on Christmas looking through the bags, pulling out designer clothes and shoes. I didn't even notice the seafood feast that was spread out on the table.

"Happy birthday my lady, I hope you like your gifts," Elijah appeared out of nowhere.

I ran and jumped up on him, wrapping my legs around his waist and kissing him all over his face. "I love it Elijah! I never had anybody do anything like this for me before. Thank you baby I love you! You're so damn slick you hid this shit good!"

I kissed him like my life depended on it without ever getting down. He sat me up on the counter and that was all she wrote. Our clothes were sprawled out all over the kitchen and the whole time we were making love I was hoping that Tiana wouldn't come downstairs and catch us in the act. After about an hour of love making we decided to eat our food which had to be warmed up by that time.

Tiana ran in the kitchen and caught me off guard once again. "Happy birthday bitch!! It's ya birthday, it's ya birthday," she sang, doing a silly dance.

I stood up and gave her a hug. "Thank you sis! You always have to be the first one to tell me," I laughed. "Did you know anything about this?" I asked.

"Well I might have known a little something but who am I to tell you?" she joked. "I knew you would love it. Elijah you're a great man to my sister."

"She's a great woman to me. Happy birthday baby," he kissed me on the cheek.

"Thank you boo, now who is down to take a shot with me for a birthday?" I asked, grabbing the Patron.

Tiana was already one step ahead of me as she went to the cabinet and grabbed three shot glasses. "I'm down!"

I poured all three of us a shot and Elijah raised his glass. "To the love of my life on her birthday," we clinked our glasses together and threw it back.

"All right y'all I'm out. I just came to wish you a happy birthday. Y'all two can get back to whatever it was that y'all were doing. I can't get too tipsy because I have to look after the kids. See y'all later!"

"Let's go for a walk," Elijah suggested and I was down.

The neighborhood we lived in was close to the city park Mt. Trashmore so we walked through a cut that led us right to the lake. The June breeze felt good against my skin as we walked around the lake holding hands.

"If I didn't believe in fairytales before I do now. I can't even express how grateful I am to have you in my life. Thank you for sticking by my side through everything I've been through. I don't know what I would have done without you," I told Elijah.

"You don't ever have to worry about being without me again. I didn't think that I was capable of loving a woman after all the shady shit I done dealt with. You proved me wrong. I love you more than I love my next breathe and I want you to be mine forever."

We walked around for over an hour before we returned back to the house. I felt like I was dreaming and at any second somebody would come and wake me up. I was living a beautiful life with a great man by my side. Things couldn't get any better.

CHAPTER SEVENTEEN
London

I had spent the entire day getting ready for my party. I started off my day with a facial and massage at the spa then I went to get a manicure and pedicure. I got some Peruvian 26 inch hair installed in my head and I thought I was the shit.

"You're gonna be late for your own party if you don't hurry up!" I heard Elijah scream from the bedroom.

"That's the point baby; I have to make a grand entrance. It's my birthday and I'm going to be the show stopper," I said while carefully applying my MAC make-up.

Elijah was throwing me an all white party at his club Paradise and I decided to wear all black. I wanted to stand out from everyone else and that was exactly what I was going to do. I always loved Elijah in all white but this time he stepped it up a notch. He had on an all white, tailor made Tom Ford suit that hugged his body and fit every inch of him perfectly. He had on some white gators and his jewelry set everything off. He had on a watch, a chain, a ring, and earrings; all gold with diamonds in them.

"Damn you looking good as hell. We're about to make these people wait a little while longer." I eyed him seductively.

"Yeah we are, especially if you keep walking around here with just your panties on. Now get dressed I have a special evening planned for you." He walked out the door and told me he would be waiting for me downstairs.

After I was sure that my make up was perfect and my hair was laid to perfection I pulled out the dress that I chose to wear. The dress fit me so tight that it looked like it was painted on and it stopped right above my knees. The top half of the dress was all mesh except for a small piece of fabric that covered my titties. There was a sexy split in the front but it didn't look slutty. I accessorized with some white gold diamond hoop earrings and matching bracelet that my man brought me. I threw on my black Jimmy Choo's and checked myself out in the mirror. When I was completely satisfied with my look I left my room.

I went into the nursery to check on my baby before I left. My mom had the nanny she hired to watch Jordan while she worked, come and keep all the kids at my house. She had all the kids sleeping so when I went in the room she put her finger up to her lips as if she was saying shhhhh.

"Let me give you my cell phone number just in case you need me. Don't hesitate to call me for anything because I will be here within ten minutes. Everything you need is in this room. Pampers and wipes over here, the milk is over th—

"Child go out and have yourself a good time. I have been taking care of babies well before you were born. Don't worry, I have everything under control sugar." The nice old lady said.

I felt good about leaving my daughter in her hands because she was great with Jordan. Leaving my baby so early wasn't the easiest thing for me to do though. I made my way downstairs before I changed my mind about going out and Elijah was waiting for me at the bottom of the stairs.

"Damn girl, you were right when you said that we might have to keep them motherfuckers waiting a little longer. I'm ready to fuck you with that dress and those heels on. You look sexy as hell baby," he kissed me on my neck.

I playfully slapped him, "We are already late now let's go before people start blowing our phones up."

He escorted me outside and in the driveway sat an all white Ashton Martin with a big red bow on it.

My eyes got wide with excitement. "Baby whose car is this?" I asked.

I turned around to see him dangling a key in front of my face. "That would be yours," he smiled like a Cheshire cat.

"Oh my God, oh my God," I snatched the keys out of his hand and tears started welling up in my eyes. "Thank you baby thank you. I don't know what I did to deserve you but I appreciate everything you do for me. This has been the best birthday I've ever had!"

"The best is yet to come, thank me later we have to go. You're going to be the first one to put miles on this car so you have to drive."

We hopped in the car and peeled off. When we got to the club Elijah paid the valet to go park our car and we walked straight to the front of the line. I felt like a celebrity as I walked on the red carpet that was rolled out just for me. People were taking pictures of Elijah and I and I heard some people screaming happy birthday to me. I got a few side eyes from some hating ass bitches but I didn't give a fuck, it was my night.

When we entered the club I spotted my family sitting over in VIP. It was my mom, Tiana, Angela, Ty, Aunt Precious, and Elijah's right hand man Ox. Everyone was dressed in all white and looking stunning. There were already bottles at the table and everyone looked like they were waiting for my arrival.

"It looks like the birthday girl just entered the building. Happy birthday London I see y'all looking like a million bucks," the DJ shouted over the music.

Everybody came and greeted me with hugs and kisses and told me happy birthday. The table at the VIP section was filled with gifts and cards and I was so overwhelmed with all the love I was getting. Two waitresses came to our table with sparklers and bottles. We had some of everything in our section from Grey Goose to Ciroc and Hennessy to Patron.

It's ya birthday, it's ya birthday

Bad bitch contest you in first place.

You in first place, you in first place,

Bad bitch contest you in first place.

2 Chains song blared through the speakers and Tiana grabbed on of my hands and Ty grabbed the other.

"Let's go bitch we're going to the dance floor!" Tiana said.

All eyes were on us when we stepped on the dance floor. We were having a good time, dancing and moving our bodies like professionals. The only time we left the dance floor was to fill our cups back up with alcohol. I was lit and so was everybody else. My mom and Angela stayed in VIP for most of the night but Elijah and Ox joined us on the dance floor. We were partying like it was 1999.

Suddenly the lights in the club got dim and a spotlight shone down on the stage.

"Can I please get the birthday girl to come to the stage? London come to the stage," the DJ said over the microphone.

I looked around at everyone because I didn't know what was going on but everybody shrugged their shoulders like they were just as clueless as me. I made my way through the crowd of people and to the stage. Elijah held my hand and helped me up the stairs that led to the stage. He led me to the area that the spotlight was shining on and when I looked down I saw everybody that was sitting in VIP standing right in front of the stage.

Elijah came and stood beside me and grabbed my hand.

"I want to thank each and every one of you for coming out to help my lady celebrate her special day," he spoke into the microphone in his hand. He then turned around to face me and looked at me with nothing but love in his eyes.

"London ever since you have come into my life I have been a better man. I never want to wake up and you're not there. Without you and Ariana my life would be pointless. I love y'all more than I love my next breath. I want to spend the rest of my life with you by my side."

I put my hand over my mouth when I saw Elijah get down on one knee and realized what was going on. "Oh my God Elijah what are you doing?" I said with tear filled eyes.

"Exactly what you think I'm doing. London Gellar will you make me the happiest man alive and be my wife?" he pulled out a box and when he opened it up I was blinded by the 7 carat diamond engagement ring. The rock was huge and it was the most beautiful piece of jewelry I ever laid eyes on.

I was now in full blown tears and didn't even care about ruining my make up anymore. "Yes Elijah, yes I will marry you!"

He put the ring on my left ring finger and we shared a long, passionate kiss. The crowd erupted in cheers and applause and the family came on the stage to share this joyous occasion with me. Elijah had a huge smile on his face when everybody came and hugged and congratulated us. Him and Ox slapped hands and gave each other some brotherly love.

"That's my best friend, that's my best friend!" Ty said.

"My baby is going to be somebody's wife. I'm so happy," my mom cried. She always got emotional when she was happy.

"I know I'm going to be your maid of honor sis we got some wedding planning to do!"

"I'll help you with any and everything daughter-in-law!" Angela said.

"Somebody finally locked my nigga down," Ox said to me as he put his arm around me and gave me a hug. "I'm happy for y'all man."

That was the best day of my life that I would remember until the day I died. I finally found true love and I was never going to let him go.

CHAPTER EIGHTEEN
The Present

I pulled up to the YMCA on Indian River Road and as soon as my feet hit the ground I noticed that the parking lot was filled with foreign cars.

"Damn I have to get me a new car," I said to myself.

It was April 16, 2015, which was a very special day for me. I strutted up to the building in my six inch heels and made my way to the room that a party was being held in.

Happy birthday to you, happy birthday to you,

Happy birthday Ariana and Caiden, happy birthday to you!

I heard everyone singing before I even entered the room. I looked through the small window of the door and looked inside before I decided to go in. There were big smiles on everyone's faces. The room was decorated with a Mickey and Minnie Mouse theme and there were two cakes with a number 1 candle on the center of both of them. My mom was holding the most handsome baby boy I ever saw, in her lap and Elijah was holding a beautiful baby girl in one arm and London was tucked under his other arm. I noticed a huge rock on her left hand and immediately got green with envy.

"Oh hell the fuck no! I know I'm not seeing what I think I'm seeing."

I didn't waste anymore time going in the party. When I walked through the door everybody stopped what they were doing and looked at me like they had seen a ghost.

"Hey everybody, did y'all miss me? I'm back and I'm here to get what's mine!" A wicked smile appeared on my face and I knew that I was about to start some shit!

to be continued...

Don't miss part 3! Text the keyword "JWP" to 22828 to get email notifications of new releases from Jessica Watkins Presents!

About the Author: Jasmine M. Williams, born and raised in Virginia Beach, VA, is a mother of two with a passion for writing. Her knack for writing started in middle school when she and a classmate used to be in competition of who could write the best short stories. Reading the novel "The Coldest Winter Ever" by Sista Souljah inspired her to want to write a story of her own. All the obstacles that life threw her way and becoming a mother at an early age didn't deter her dreams; it made her fight harder to make them a reality. She aspires to become a full time author and to see one or more of her books hit the silver screen. While she is writing and being a full time mother, she is also working on getting her Bachelor's degree in Business Management.

23416552R00127

Made in the USA
Middletown, DE
25 August 2015